Savage
DEVIL

Green Hills Academy Trilogy

Book 1

Josie Max

SAVAGE DEVIL

For information contact :
Josie Max at josiemax@josiemaxwrites.com
http://www.josiemaxwrites.com

Cover design by Josie Max
ISBN: 978-1-955184-00-7

First Edition: March 2021

978-1-955184-00-7

CONTENTS

PROLOGUE

Violet

COLD. THE NIGHT BIT into my skin like jagged ice, sending shivers through my body.

The worn T-shirt with a smiley face I wore with fleece pajama pants weren't enough to keep away the chill of the April morning. Maybe it wasn't the air, but the sight of my mother's bloated body being dragged from the pond.

I frowned.

Happy Pond was rather big. Large enough to drown in.

A local hangout for teens, and one of them found my mom. At least, that's what the officer told me.

There's nothing happy about this place.

I pulled the coarse, gray blanket the officer gave me tighter. My teeth chattered anyway, as if they knew something I didn't.

"Oh, doll, you don't need to see this." The officer, a woman with kind eyes, wrapped an arm around me, guiding me farther inland. "The ambulance will be here soon. They're going to want to check you out."

We walked, but I said nothing. The time filled with her sweet ramblings.

"I'm Officer Janet Harris, but you can call me Janet." Her grin wrinkled the corners of her eyes. "You go to school nearby?"

I shook my head. I wasn't from this part of town. Where I lived, finding bodies wasn't so unusual. You'd be surprised how many dead people wound up near the trailer park. Maybe that's why I was shaking. The shock that my mom would be anywhere near the gilded elite that made up North Green Hills; her lifeless body floating in their happy pond.

A year ago, I wouldn't have been shocked if my mom's body was found in an unusual location. It wasn't like she lived a perfect life. The only thing that made her happy most of her life was drugs and guys with guns.

Despite my mom's not-so clean decisions, I loved her.

But the difference between last year and this, was that she tried to get clean. Determined to make sobriety stick. I was proud of her. She had worked so hard. This shouldn't have been her end and it ripped me apart that I couldn't help her.

I sat on a damp wooden bench near a playground, the pond had disappeared.

"Want some coffee? I got some decaf." Officer Harris' tone dripped with pity as I looked up. The moon broke free from the clouds, making a halo around her head.

"Yes. Thank you." I found my voice. It was groggy, but there.

She glanced around and we both saw a tall, older man heading our way, his eyes squarely on me. My mom would have called him distinguished. I swallowed, trying to ease my queasy stomach. Something about the way he stared made me wonder if I was in trouble.

But for what? Do they think I killed my mother?

"Mayor, I hadn't expected to see you here," the officer said to the man in the long black woolen coat.

"Officer Harris, nice to see you again." He flashed the whitest smile I had ever seen. "Knight found the body."

Janet's eyes slid to me. I knew that look. She was worried I'd either burst into tears or brandish a fist. She was wise to monitor me. I wasn't immune to throwing a punch or two when someone thought it would be fun to push my buttons.

But witnessing my mother's damp gray body pulled from the pond drained any energy I had. There was no anger during the predawn light, the only thing I felt was empty and alone.

"I look forward to the Officer's Ball this year at your place, mayor." She nodded at him.

"Of course. It's a yearly tradition." His smile didn't reach his eyes.

"Why don't we speak closer to my car, mayor?" She waved him away before turning to me. "I'll go get that coffee for you."

I blinked. A nod felt like too much energy. A wave of exhaustion took over and despite the small puddle on the bench, I laid down. Perhaps closing my eyes for a minute would help. Maybe it was all a dream . . . a nightmare. When I opened them again, my mom would fry up some bacon with a Virginia Slim cigarette between her fingers and a smile on her face.

Bacon and my mom humming her

favorite Nirvana tune consumed my thoughts as I drifted away. But right before I let go of the terrible events that led me to this hard, wet bench, I heard the mayor announce, “I’ll take care of her.”

ONE

Violet

Five Months Later

"THE WATERMELON ISN'T BAD." Aunt Dahlia's berry-nude lips tipped into a grin so big it wrinkled the corner of her eyes. She had never looked more beautiful.

I didn't hold back my frown.

"Yuck. I'll stick with my chocolate

peanut butter milkshake, thank you very much." I gave her my best smug smile. "I meant it as a joke. You didn't have to actually get the watermelon milkshake."

We were seated outside the milkshake shop in the Green Hills National Airport. I hadn't been to any other airport in my life, but according to Aunt Dahlia, they all look the same.

The *Milk Shack* had several locations around town, but we came to the airport to get our custom-made milkshakes today.

She reached across the tall, round table and gripped my hand. "I know. But I'm not afraid of trying new things."

The florescent light that hung over our table caused Dahlia's green eyes to sparkle. Her smile faded and I knew what she was trying to do. It was the same expression my mom always gave me when she tried to teach me a lesson.

My mom also had the same green eyes; in fact, I was the only Adler female with brown eyes. They were from my dad, but he had never been in my life—I didn't even know his name.

As a seventeen-year-old, it was imperative to react as any self-respecting teenager should when an adult was dolling out wisdom. So, I rolled my eyes.

But this time the eye-roll came with a tear.

"I'll only be a phone call away."

I snorted, irritated that she was leaving me. "Don't you know? Nobody makes calls anymore."

"Oh, well, I'm so glad you told me. I would have thoroughly embarrassed myself by wanting to talk to my only niece, the one I love with all my heart . . . while she got to live in a mansion with the mayor."

I stirred the milkshake and shrugged off her words. "I don't understand why I can't live with you for my senior year of high school? I'll be eighteen in three weeks and—"

She held up her hand. "Violet, stop, please. You know this doesn't make me happy. I don't want to be away from you, either. But it makes sense."

I folded my arms over my chest, mumbling, "For you."

Dahlia let out a sigh. "Not for me. For *you*. When would you have a chance like this ever again in your life? Last I checked, we don't have a mysterious wealthy relative who left us all their money in a will. The mayor was nice enough to take you in for your senior year of high school and pay for you to go to Green Hills Academy."

I bit my lip and refused to look her

way. "That doesn't mean I have to go. If I can be with you, then I'll happily give up living in a fancy home and the privileged life that comes with it."

Why was the mayor being so helpful? Sure, his nephew found me by the pond the night my mom died. And for some weird reason, the mayor showed up and got all in my business. But didn't he have more important things to worry about . . . like, I don't know, running a town.

Dahlia leaned closer. "But I would rarely be home. Whether you like it or not, my job requires a lot of travel. You just lost you mom—" her voice cracked and she paused, clearing her throat. "You need people around you. I wish I could take time from work to look after you, but I can't. The mayor promised you'd be well cared for. Besides, you'll be the first person to get out of the South Side Trailer Park and get to move to the North Side."

That wasn't exactly true. But my aunt had never heard of the story of the girl who managed to snag a rich guy from the north side and got out. My mom told me she had known her when she was a teenager.

"I don't know him and he doesn't know me. What if he's a serial killer or drug kingpin or—"

"Stop." Dahlia stepped down from her stool and came to my side, placing her hand gently on my shoulder. "He's the mayor of Green Hills. I doubt he has time for killing." She added a wink to make me smile.

It wouldn't work. Being left with strangers by the only family I had left was all I thought about. I met him once. Something felt off about him on that early morning of my mom's overdose at Happy

Pond. Maybe I was acting ridiculous, pretending he might be a serial killer or drug pusher, but I didn't want to live with him and his family.

I wanted my aunt.

She was the person I always called when my mom went out looking for drugs. I remembered countless weekends staying up late watching movies and eating popcorn with her. She wasn't so much an aunt as a second mother.

"Besides, didn't you tell me you wanted to get into Winter River University? With a year at Green Hills Academy and your GPA, I bet you would have a shot."

I raised my eyes from the beige tiled floor. "You think?"

She shrugged. "Much better chance than continuing at your old high school. Besides, I bet if you didn't give the mayor any trouble, he might write you a letter of recommendation for the university. You'd be sure to be invited to apply."

I lifted my thumb, nibbling on my thumbnail, taking in what she was saying.

I first heard about Winter River University from my mom two years ago. She was high on whatever drug she got a hold of at the moment fiddling with that locket of hers that she always wore, but I remember her getting serious and pointing at me. She told me only the elite got into Winter River. That if I ever wanted to get out of the South Green Hills Trailer Park and get a chance at something real in life, I needed to get into that school. That it was a hidden secret among the wealthy and they didn't want just anyone going there.

She said, *"If you want to beat the wealthy oppressors at their own game, you go there. Do whatever you can to get into that school."*

I assumed she was hallucinating. If it was that great, why had I never heard of it before?

Then I looked it up and it seemed nice, if not pricey. Then I read a few blog posts on various websites that all said the same thing—it was an elite school the rich didn't want the public to know about. Their hidden gem.

It's so exclusive that they only invite a select number of people to apply. And there's no guarantee that if you get to apply to the school that you'd be accepted.

That's when I became obsessed. I maintained straight A's and did as many extracurriculars as possible. I volunteered at soup kitchens and nursing homes.

Even with all that, I knew the only way I could get in was with a scholarship. Unfortunately, the university only accepted five scholarship students a year.

Despite my perfect GPA and everything I had done to get a chance at being accepted by Winter River, I knew there was a slim chance I'd get in.

Until now.

"You're strong and the smartest person I know. I wish I had been there for your mom when she called me, but I was here with zero cell reception." Dahlia waved a hand around the airport.

Heartbreak added lines to her face, and I knew she blamed herself for Mom's death.

"It wasn't your fault, Aunt Dahlia." I hopped off my stool and pulled her into a hug.

"Why was she at that pond anyway? She hated ponds, lakes, anything to do with a lot of water," my aunt muttered into my shoulder.

She smelled like Mom. I smiled,

remembering Mom not having enough money at Christmas to get Aunt Dahlia a nice gift, so she wrapped some of the drug store perfume she had bought herself. It was cheap. Mom couldn't afford anything better, but that didn't stop Dahlia from wearing it.

The only thing I had from my mom was the bracelet she gave me on my sixteenth birthday. It was cheap but it was from her. Only if the police had found her locket. Then I'd actually have something of hers. Something I knew *she* loved.

I guess they never found it.

"I may not be the reason Rose died, but I should have been there for her." She sighed and pulled me back, staring into my eyes. "I thought she had cleaned up her act. If something was going on, you could have told me."

"She had. That's what I don't

understand. She was so excited to get her one-year chip at the NA meeting that coming Sunday. I don't understand what happened . . .. I even talked to her sponsor and she told me mom was her usual self, nothing out of the ordinary."

We had a fight that night. About my father and why I never knew him. Maybe that's why she was about to go on a drug bender, drug her own daughter, and then drown herself.

I remember the feeling of being groggy that night but until the people at the hospital took my blood and tested me, I never realized she would have drugged me. She had never done anything like that before.

Her lips thinned. I could tell it made little sense to Dahlia. I wasn't the only one with questions and guilt.

She shook her head and tucked some

strands of my dark locks behind my ear. "If there was something out of the ordinary, the police would've picked up on it. Let's focus on your future right now. You have a chance to go to an elite school and live in luxury for a while."

I shrugged. Yeah, that was amazing, but it felt empty without Mom to share it with me.

"I think it's weird the mayor wants to help."

Dahlia nodded. "It's kind of strange, but you know those political types. He's probably doing it because he thinks it will help him get reelected in November. His publicist probably told him to help the down-on-her-luck girl by paying for her to go to Green Hills Academy and take her in."

"But what if he doesn't get elected again? Does that mean I'll be out on my ass come Thanksgiving?"

"Of course not," Dahlia said, but the crease between her brows told me she wasn't so sure.

A voice came over the loudspeaker and Dahlia turned to grab her purse from the table. She pulled out her ticket and said, "That's my flight. I have to get going as they're boarding soon. Still need to get through security. One last hug and then you call me tomorrow to tell me how your first day of school went."

She threw her arms wide and I hugged her tight. I felt like I was five again, afraid of my mom leaving my room at night, that the monster under my bed might appear once she was gone.

"The mayor said there would be a car out front of baggage claim to pick you up."

I nodded, too emotional to respond.

She pulled back and brushed a tear

from her cheek.

"You're a beautiful, smart, and tough girl, Violet Adler. You haven't had the best life, but here you are. I know you won't let anything or anyone beat you down. Us Adler women have too much spice in our blood to dissolve into nothing."

I chuckled through my tears.

"Mom always said that, too."

"And our mom said it to us. Because it's true. I wish I could accompany you to the mayor's place, but I have to head off to Boise for work."

For me, at this moment, Boise, Idaho sounded glorious compared to a mansion.

"I'll, uh . . . miss you." I whispered with my head down.

"I'll miss you too, Violet. I bet you'll make friends right away and have a cute boyfriend by the end of the week."

"Ugh, it's not that easy, Aunt Dahlia." I

shook my head.

Adults always believed kids could make friends with a snap of their fingers. It's like they thought we were all three years old and would play with a potato if it could talk.

She gave my arm a squeeze as she shrugged her bag up on her shoulder. "I know. I'm just, uh . . .. I just love you."

I frowned. If she loved me, then why was she leaving me?

TWO

Violet

MY HEART BEAT WILDLY in my chest as I stared at the large home outside the car.

The car ride to the mayor's home was insane to begin with, and now it stopped in front of something that looked like the

Queen of England might step out any minute.

The door swung open and the driver, dressed in a black suit, stood there and gazed ahead.

He hadn't said a word to me the entire time. I wondered if he couldn't speak. My imagination ran away with me on the car ride, and I wondered if the mayor had permanently removed the vocal cords from all his servants like some evil dictator who demanded silence.

I shook my head. My mom wasn't perfect, but she had taught me to be strong. To move toward fear with strength and dignity, because if I didn't, then fear would eat away at me.

"Don't be a wilting tulip, be a thorny rose." I sometimes wondered if she told me those things so I would do what she never could—fight back. She let drugs beat her,

but I wouldn't let her death, or this unknown family, get to me.

I pushed my foot onto the pavement and stood tall. Jetting my chin out, I gazed over at the driver.

"You are to meet the Mr. King in the back of the house," the man said.

I blinked. *So his vocal cords were intact.*

He waved toward the pathway that led around the house. Flowering plants and bushes edged the large slate tiles of the pathway, and I was sure there would be a bench hidden somewhere along the way. I gazed up as I walked and was surprised at the height of the mayor's home. It seemed like a two-story home from the front, but I counted four rows of windows on the side.

The house was made of large, beige bricks that appeared rough to the touch. I never realized bricks came in any other color than red. But then again, I grew up in a trailer park where the only bricks were holding up cars without wheels.

There was a large, wooden door attached to a fence and as I reached for the black iron latch, it opened. There, on the other side, stood the driver's doppelganger, and I gasped and took a step back. "No, we're not twins; in fact, we're not even related. I'm Theodore, the butler, Ms. Adler."

He was a lot more talkative than his non-twin.

"I didn't mean to stare. I'm sorry if—"

Theodore waved me off. "No apology necessary. We get it all the time. Mr. King is this way. Just follow me."

I nodded and stepped through the gate. My mouth fell open when I took in the backyard. It wasn't so much a yard as an acre or more. There were large, rolling gardens that slopped downhill, and a deck and gazebo that seemed as if they were hovering over a small stream.

And directly behind the house was a large pool, sauna, and a second, miniature version of the mayor's home.

Theodore walked around the pool and waved me to the front door of the smaller home.

"The mayor and his guests are directly inside the pool house."

I didn't believe my mouth could fall open any further, but it did. "D-did you say . . . the *pool* house?"

This was a pool house? It looked like it belonged on a suburban street, not next to a pool.

"Yes." He opened the white door when I moved closer. "They are all in the living room."

"Thanks," I mumbled as I became

hypnotized by the opulence.

Not only was the exterior outrageous, but the interior was like something from a high-end décor magazine. Mom used to buy those magazines when she had the extra cash—not because she thought she could fix up our trailer to match those pictures, but to imagine she'd lived like that. It was pure fantasy and here I was, stepping into her dream.

The floors were dark hardwood, and the walls were stark white with frame molding. Everything was bold. Black wooden furniture, deep blue velvet chairs and couches. Gold and white accent pieces. A modern take on the old world.

My fingers slid across the black table by the front door. Not a bit of dust or a nick in that wood. I doubt there was anything second-hand in the place.

A throat cleared and I turned to

discover a woman, not much older than me, with bright red staining her thin lips and platinum blond hair pulled back into a tight bun. Her perfectly sculpted brow rose. "Did you get lost?"

"No."

"Ms. Adler. There's one thing you should know about Mr. King. He doesn't tolerate tardiness. It shows a blatant disrespect for others. He understands that you recently lost a relative, so he'll let this pass . . . just this once."

A relative? She's acting like my third cousin twice removed just died, not the woman who raised me.

My jaw tensed as I did my best to bite back the *blatant disrespect* I wanted to throw her way.

"How do you know I'm Ms. Adler?" I spat out, not at all hiding my irritation.

Despite my obvious anger at the bitch,

she clapped back.

Her eyes slid up and down my body with a smirk. "You can't be serious. I heard you are from South Green Hills. And judging by your clothing, you would fit in perfectly at a South Green Hills barbecue."

I glanced down at my clothes. My jean shorts were ripped and not in the stylish way—more so in the 'I bought them two years ago and they were one of the two pairs I owned'. Then I noticed the stain on my T-shirt from the milkshake.

I pursed my lips. "You caught me. I'm Violet Adler. Guess there's no fooling the fashion police."

I slid my eyes down her body just as she did me and smirked. I may have bought my clothes at a store with the word 'outlet' in the name, but it didn't mean I lacked taste. She wanted to judge me; well, I was going to judge her right back.

"I'm Ms. Peterson, Mr. King's private assistant. When he is at his private residence, I keep track of his schedule and who is to see him and who is not." She took a breath and was obviously incapable of smiling. "Now that we've established who we both are, let's get you where you need to be, which is the conference. The mayor is meeting with journalists in the living room."

Conference? Is that what rich people called talking?

As she walked down the hall, she said, "We've taken care of your clothing. You won't have to worry about wearing those rags anymore."

Rags? Ms. Peterson was laying it on thick. Did she think we were in a Dickens novel? What in the fresh hell was wrong with her?

"Thank goodness." I stopped in the hall

and rested my hand against my forehead. "My tatters are so itchy," I said with a snort.

We stopped in front of two double doors and she turned to me. "Of course, they are. That's why they're cheap. Now, Mr. King will do all the talking. Don't worry, you don't have to say anything about your horrible time in South Green Hills," she said the last part with a sneer.

Wow. She really believed the garbage that was coming out of her mouth.

"Right." I side-eyed her as I turned to the door.

She pulled the doors apart and they slid straight into the wall.

Inside the room, which was about ten times bigger than my trailer, was the mayor in a navy blazer and peach-colored button-up shirt standing on the far side by a fireplace. Next to him stood an overly Botoxed and collagen-filled woman with long blond hair. A dozen people with cameras filled half the room.

"And here is the girl of the hour, Ms. Violet Adler," the mayor said with that bright, white smile I remember from Happy Pond. Even in the light, it was blinding.

Flashes went off and for a moment, I couldn't see anything. I felt a pair of hands on my arms, pulling me farther into the room.

"Please, ya'll, give her some space. She's been through so much," a woman with a thick, southern accent said as she guided me closer to the fireplace.

I blinked until my sight came back. It was Botox woman. She tried to grin at me, but it appeared painful and looked more like a grimace.

"My wife Kiki and I knew the moment we heard of the horrific events at Happy

Pond that we had to embrace this young girl. Take her in and help her heal." The mayor placed his hand on my shoulder and squeezed it a little too firmly.

I gazed up at him to find him staring at me, his eyes blank. It was chilling. Sure, he was smiling, but it was like he wasn't looking at me, but through me.

An icy shiver ran down my spine. No, I wasn't cold. I was sweating in the overstuffed room. A desperate need to get out and run back to the airport filled me.

I already missed Aunt Dahlia. This was the mayor's home, and I didn't know a soul. I had no friends here.

I never thought I would say this, but I missed South Green Hills Trailer Park. Some of my neighbors weren't good people, but most were nice and worked hard to survive. But even the worst person at the park would never glare at me the way the mayor just did.

I swallowed and tried my best to appear happy to be there. If the mayor wanted me in his home for publicity, then I'd give him what he wanted. Later, I could ask him about a recommendation letter.

Whatever it took, my mom had told me in the past. That's what I had to do.

I felt a gentler touch on my arm by Kiki. She may look like Barbie with a bad face lift, but I bet she was nice. She must be for taking me in, having never met me and all.

"Oh, dear, you're shivering. Here, take this." She reached over and on a hook by the fireplace was a pink blanket.

I wasn't cold, but I took her offering. The blanket was the softest thing I had ever touched in my life.

"As you can see, Violet needs her rest. My press secretary can answer the rest of your questions. Let this young girl have some peace," the mayor said to the group.

Some flashes went off as the journalists took pictures of us.

"Mr. Mayor, just one last question, please." A tall woman leaned forward with her recording device.

"Fine. One more, but then that's it."

"Two years ago, your brother and his wife were killed in a plane crash off the coast of Cape Cod, along with your long-time friend Mr. Jack Franklin. Then you took in your brother's children . . .."

"Yes. My nephew Knight, and my niece Ava. How is this a question?"

"I'm getting to that. Now you're taking in a girl you don't even know. For a man who never had kids, you seem to like to scoop up other's children."

Kiki gasped.

"Are you implying that these children

are property, to be plucked up when the owners have died?"

The reporter's eyes widened. She shook her head. "No, t-that's not what I meant. What I meant to say was—"

"I think you've said enough. Please leave. They're human beings, not *things*." The mayor narrowed his eyes at the woman.

She nodded and stepped back. After a few minutes, all the people in the room had left except for the mayor and his wife.

He turned to me with his haunting stare. "Please accept my apology, Violet."

"It's fine. I think she just messed up what she meant to say."

"That's not an excuse." His eyes slid down and landed on my chest before quickly rising to meet my gaze once more. "Ms. Ellis hates me. Her questions have always been farcical at best. It's like she has a vendetta against me. But that's the price I pay being the mayor."

"I am meeting Janice at the club for dinner," Kiki said as she walked to the sliding doors.

"Thank you for the blanket. It's super soft."

The moment Kiki turned her sights on me, she sneered. "Is it? Oh, is it *super* soft? That's just super," she said in a mocking, baby tone.

She turned on her white stiletto heels and yelled back as she went down the hall, "This better be worth it, Ichabod. I already have to live with the other brats. I better get a raise for all this . . . uh, mothering."

I heard the door slam as she left. So much for her being nice.

"I guess we're alone now." The mayor stared at my chest and walked toward me.

I backed away until my neck hit the

mantel of the fireplace.

"Oh, look . . . there's nowhere else for you to go." His lips curled as he placed his hands on either side of my head.

THREE

Violet

I COULDN'T MOVE MY head. My stomach felt like I had recently ingested a boulder. I knew the guy was creepy, but not like that much. My eyes darted around the room. We really were alone. Even if I screamed, would anyone hear?

I was standing in his pool house. He probably paid his servants enough to ignore the screams of a young girl.

"You know, the last guy who tried to do this to me winded up in jail." I wasn't about to give up without a fight.

He threw his head back in laughter. "I'm the fucking mayor. No one's going to arrest me." He ran his hands through his thick brown hair that grayed at the temples.

The man was handsome with a rugged, square jawline, and that seemed to make all this worse. The mayor had everything—power, money, looks, and I bet he had been coddled because of it.

He looked like one of those men who had never been told no. Until now.

But much to my surprise, Mayor King stepped back and shrugged after his laughter died.

"After what you've been through," his eyes slid to me as if waiting for me to react, but I kept my stance firm, "I suppose I should give you some time. But there is an order of things and in this house—"

I folded my arms. "The pool house?"

His jaw tightened and he firmly took hold of my chin. "Listen here, you brat. I pay for everything in this place. I paid for your schooling, for your clothes, for your life. Don't think for one minute I won't take it all back, and you can go find out what happened to that garbage can you called a home."

My heart sank as his words became clear.

"You mean the trailer?"

His grip loosened. That same cold shiver that I always got when I was in his presence slid down my spine and his finger trailed down my neck. "Oh, not just the trailer, Violet. Think bigger. That's the difference between you and me." He smirked before he continued, "Where I'm from, we are always several steps ahead. We don't just get a job to pay the bills, we buy the whole fucking company. So, when I say what happened to your home, I don't just mean that terrible trailer . . . I mean the whole park."

I swallowed and tried to hold back my frown. He wanted to frighten me. I knew enough about men like the mayor—big guys who got their kicks from intimidating others to get what they wanted.

He would not break me that easily.

"You bought the trailer park?"

He considered me for a minute, his tone condescending. "You're not as dumb as I thought. But it's not just the park I bought, but the land. And all the surrounding properties."

Of course, he'd be a shitty landlord. The moment he strolled up to the officer at Happy Pond, I knew he was a dick. It was a feeling then, a sixth sense, but now I had proof.

Living with the mayor was a bad idea. Once Aunt Dahlia found out, she wouldn't want me living here, even if it meant losing out on attending Green Hills Academy.

Yeah, I wanted to get a chance at getting into Winter River University next year, but not if it meant living with a psycho for the next few months.

I held my hands up. "Look, I can tell you and your wife don't want me here. Why don't I do you both a favor and leave? You can return the clothes and get back the money for the school."

I tossed the blanket to the floor and tried to step around him. The mayor reached out and wrapped his fingers tightly around my arm. I winced as he shoved me back until my head hit the mantel.

"Once you stepped foot on my property, you became mine. I own you, little girl. And if you want a chance at getting into Winter River University, you'll live here and do as I say. You'll go to Green Hills Academy tomorrow and be the demure, thankful bitch I expect you to be."

My eyes flickered to the doorway. There was a shadow in the hall. A servant maybe? Or perhaps that stuck-up bitch of an assistant I met when I first walked in, Ms. Peterson. Either way, I prayed whoever it was would interrupt.

But the shadow never moved, and I

wondered if it wasn't a person but maybe just a shadow of a statue or a table.

I was on my own. No aunt to help me or Kiki or even the mayor's nephew who found me at the pond.

"How did you find out I wanted to go to Winter River?" I asked slowly.

His grip never relented as he lifted his head, gazing at himself in the mirror above the mantel. "I had the best conversation with your aunt yesterday. She's so sweet, not at all like . . . well, never mind. She told me so much about you. I feel like you could be my daughter. Don't you want to be daddy's good little girl?"

His hand cupped my cheek as his thumb pressed my bottom lip until my mouth opened.

I slapped his hand away. "It's not as if I have to go to Winter River. That's not the only university in the country."

"You're right." He let go of my arm. The mayor turned and walked to the doorway until he glanced back at me. "There's so many colleges and universities, too many to count really." He tilted his head as if deep in thought. "I wonder what would happen if I sent a letter to everyone you applied to and told them how I tried to help you, but you gave me nothing but trouble. That you were too much like your mother and I worried you would OD, too." He paused. "Certainly, universities would have to reconsider the risk, no matter your grades."

No. Oh God, no. I glanced around, looking for an escape. Something to get me out of the hole I was being dug farther and farther into. But there was nothing. More importantly, there was no one but me and him. A rich, powerful man who had the respect of other rich and powerful people. And me, a nobody from nowhere.

It was David and Goliath, but I had no stone and no slingshot.

I could tell Dahlia. She'd know what to do.

I was about to tell him to take his orders and shove them up his tiny dickhole when he appeared to read my mind.

"That aunt of yours is so nice. It would be a shame if she lost her job. I went golfing with James Tikon, the CEO of *Tikon Industries*, and I told him I was helping Dahlia's niece." His eyes landed on me with the same stony stare he had at the pond.

That was where she worked. *Tikon Industries.*

Images of my aunt and I laughing over milkshakes just hours ago flashed in my head. It seemed like years had passed since then.

I could run away. Pretend I was okay with everything and grab a few things from this place. I would pawn them if I had to—they had money and could easily replace anything I took. I was sure the artwork on the walls was worth something.

I never thought I would consider stealing. Even when my mom used what little money we had for drugs, I always had a can of beans stashed away in the woods. I made sure I kept anything important in a secret place in the woods near the trailer park.

But with that kind of threat, I'd steal to get out of it. I refused to let that man hurt me or my aunt.

"There's no point to fight this, little girl. Unless you do what I say, your sweet aunt will suffer and you'll never get a higher education. You and your kind will remain struggling until the day you die."

My kind. He meant anyone who wasn't wealthy.

"What is it you want me to do?" I asked with a sigh, realizing there was no way out.

His lips curled, causing the corner of his gray eyes to wrinkle. "That's my good little girl."

FOUR

Violet

I STOOD OUT FRONT of the mayor's home in my school uniform. Ms. Peterson barged into my room at six o'clock this morning to wake me. I was picked and prodded and combed so much my skin vibrated from the abuse.

As I discovered from Ms. Peterson when she interrupted the mayor before he could tell me what he wanted me to do for him yesterday, the whole pool house was mine to live in until the end of the school year.

That was a relief. It would be a nightmare to live under the same roof as that psycho, mafia-king wannabe.

The pool house had two bedrooms, each with their own bathroom. There was a full kitchen with beige granite counters and dark wooden cabinets.

Ms. Peterson apologized for the outdated décor. I laughed when she said that, assuming she was joking. Apparently, she was not. These people were on a different level of reality. Everything looked gorgeous and expensive. I hated them, but I loved that pool house.

I had yet to see the inside of the

mayor's home. From what I witnessed of the mayor and his wife yesterday, I had no desire to ever step foot in their home.

"The ladies should be here any minute," Ms. Peterson said with a curt nod.

She looked just like she had yesterday. Her hair pulled back in a tight bun, red lips, and a dark suit that was fashionable yet understated.

"So, they all ride together to school?"

I was told by Ms. Peterson that I would get a ride from the local girls. They were all seniors who went to Green Hills Academy.

"Yes. Their families live in the neighborhood. Young mister Knight dates Seraphina. I'm sure you both will have much to talk about." Her gaze slid down the back of my outfit.

I rolled my eyes. "I'm wearing the uniform you gave me. There's nothing 'outlet' about it. I've been plucked like a chicken and painted like a—"

Ms. Peterson held up her hand to stop me. "There will be no foul language in the mayor's home."

I bit my lip to prevent me from pointing out that we weren't standing in his home, but in his driveway. And the way the mayor treated me yesterday, I doubted profanity was high on his list of concerns.

I rolled my eyes and shuffled. "Whatever."

I liked the uniform. It reminded me of something from Clueless, but blue and black instead of yellow and black. It had a very 90s feel to it. Even the wealthy could afford cute uniforms.

They had pulled my hair back into the tightest, smoothest ponytail I had ever worn in my life. There was a hairdresser brought in and a makeup artist—because of course there was. I was told they worked with Kiki and she was gracious enough to lend them to me.

I tried hard not to gag when the makeup artist and hairdresser gushed about Kiki's generosity.

I heard a car rev and looked up to a red sporty car followed by a black SUV and then a silver sedan pulling into the driveway. They circled around the large fountain and the door to the red car popped open.

A girl that was my age stepped out. She had long blond hair that fell all the way down her back and a crimson fur capelet over her uniform. But it was her tits that caught my eye. You would have to be blind not to notice them. They looked unusually big and utterly fake.

Her pale pink lips frowned as she slid

her sunglasses down her nose, staring at me.

She lifted her hand and waved. "Hi, Ms. Peterson, this must be Violet. I'm so glad to be taking her to school today." Her voice was bubbling with enthusiasm.

"Seraphina, lovely to see you as always. I told Violet you would have lots to talk about." She nodded at me and turned back toward the house, leaving me alone with the fur-caped, gargantuan-tittied Barbie.

I held up my hand and waved at Seraphina. "Hi, it's nice to meet you. Am I riding with you?"

Once Ms. Peterson had stepped into the house, Seraphina's mega-watt smile fell. "Unfortunately. When you sit, don't mess up the leather." She flicked her gaze up and down my body and her lip curled. "I understand that trailer trash can stain."

What the hell? I just met her, and she

was already attacking me.

It went from bad to worse in North Green Hills.

I sighed and opened the door, throwing my backpack onto the floorboard of the front passenger seat. Sliding into the cream leather seat, it surprised me at how comfortable it was considering the size.

"You have a nice car."

I pulled the door closed and Seraphina started the engine. My head jerked back as she slammed her foot on the gas.

"It's a specially designed Mercedes that Daddy just had to get me. I wouldn't accept anything else. There are Swarovski crystals in the headlights, that's how you know it's quality." The corner of her pink lips curled.

"Okay." I nodded because what do you say to that? "So, is there a nickname you go by or a shortened version of you name?"

I decided I'd give her a pass for the trailer trash remark. Rich people always had their heads filled with nonsense about anyone who wasn't part of the top three percent. I found if you just took time to get to know someone, they weren't as bad as they first appeared.

Except for the mayor. He was creepy.

"It's Seraphina. Ser-a-phin-a," she said, raising her voice.

"I'm not hard of hearing," I grumbled.

She tilted her head and gave me a sad look. "Of course not. I know you've been through some stuff. What Knight told me, it's just . . . ugh, I couldn't imagine."

I knew there was a heart under all that fur and plastic. Just took some conversation and I knew she wasn't as bad as she first let on.

"Thanks. Yeah, the past several months

have been tough."

"I'd kill myself if I had a mother like that. I mean, seriously? Were you held in that trailer against your will?"

My eyes widened as I stared at her. She'd kill herself? Who the fuck talked like that?

"No . . ." I said slowly, "she was my mother."

Seraphina grimaced as if she ate some bad fish. "It's lucky she died, then. Now you don't have to worry about that shit life she gave you. And then Knight rescued you. He's the best. Such a hero. My hero." She pressed her hand to her heart and sighed.

"Your hero? But he rescued me."

Her nostrils flared. "I know, stupid. Thank fuck you're getting a better education at Green Hills Academy. I can't imagine what sort of backward things you were learning at public school," she sneered as she said the last two words.

I played with the charms on my bracelet. "I got straight A's."

My mom got the bracelet for me for my birthday two years ago and for some stupid reason, I thought it would give me luck today. But it's not working as I was already dealing with a stuck-up bitch and I wasn't even at school yet.

I narrowed my eyes at her. What. A. Snob.

"Yeah, but A's at public school are like C's at the Academy. I get B's so technically, I'm smarter than you. Anyway, the reason I said Knight was my hero is because he's my boyfriend."

"Okay."

Perhaps it was best if I just nodded and ignored the ignorant shit that spewed out of her mouth. I was positive she had a heart in her chest, but it appeared malnourished.

"I'm serious, Violet." She took her eyes off the road for a moment to glare at me before turning back and almost driving off the pavement. "Knight and I have a history. There's a hierarchy at Green Hills. Knight and I are the king and queen of the school. Then there are our friends; they're like the aristocracy. And then there's the rest of the school . . .."

I rolled my lips together, trying to hold back my laugher. "And where do I fit in?" This girl was so conceited, it was hilarious.

"You're a, uh, what did they call it way back when? Oh, I know. You're a serf."

"Wow. Good to know." I nodded seriously, still holding back my grin.

"Look, I'm doing you a favor. Now you know that you can't be seen with us. And as for Knight and his crew, just stay away.

You may want to go up and thank him for saving you, but you're nothing to him. Okay? Try to think of it like your walking on the sidewalk and you walk around an ant. The ant doesn't matter to you, but you don't want to kill it needlessly."

She compared me to a serf and an ant. If everyone at the school was like her, my senior year was going to be the worst year of my life.

"Knight and I will graduate and then go to Winter River University together next year. Its almost a given we both get in; both our parents went. It's expected."

I wish I were that lucky. What I wouldn't give to go there. What I'm giving up to *hopefully* go there . . ..

I nodded and turned to look out the window. It's not like I had many friends back at my old school. Studying hard meant I couldn't hang out much with people.

But I had a couple of close friends—Jenni and Kyle. They were bookworms like me. Kyle lived in the trailer park with me, but Jenni lived down the road in a townhouse. I thought her place was huge until I saw the mayor's pool house.

Maybe I could invite them over. My heart gave a jump at the thought. I needed some friends now. Being surrounded with cold, shallow, movie-villain wannabes wasn't my idea of happiness. Even with all the fancy clothes and beautiful surroundings.

The car came to a stop and I realized we had pulled up in front of what looked like a castle. It was made of gray stones and there were several towers. *Towers.*

The door opened and a man in a bow tie that matched my skirt waved me out. I grabbed my backpack and hopped out.

I watched as Seraphina ignored the man who bowed to her before he took her place behind the wheel.

"Oh my God, they have valet parking?"

Seraphina's brow creased. "Yes. This isn't a garbage school like where you went." She chuckled.

I noticed the girls who were in the other cars that had followed us here saddled up to Seraphina and joined her in laughter. Each looked like a different version of Barbie. Seraphina was blond Barbie, then there was Barbie with long raven hair, and the other with light auburn hair.

There was another set of laughter that came from the other side of the cars. It was deeper and fueled with testosterone. I glanced over to a group of guys. All of them smiling, except for the one in the middle.

He wove his fingers through his inky waves. My mouth went dry. His eyes, a wintry gray, narrowed as they raked over my body. The way he stared felt like a knife had slid straight into my heart. As if my heart was meant to be pierced all along and finally found the blade that belonged there.

He stood tall among his group of friends, but they were all big. He was gorgeous from his fitted black uniform pants to his blazer and tie, which was casually loosened.

I was seventeen. Seeing guys in anything resembling a suit did nothing to me. But on him, it hit me in all the right places.

"Knight. Hey, babe. I was hoping I'd see you this morning." Seraphina's voice rose until she sounded like a child. It was both revolting and irritating, like listening to nails on a chalkboard while someone puked in your lap.

His cool gaze slid to her before returning to me. Seraphina noticed that too because you would have to be deaf not to hear her growl as she cut a glare to me.

"She looks like lots of fun. Maybe we can play with her at lunch," one guy with short blond hair who stood near Knight said.

He was hot, too. They all were. Perfectly chiseled cheekbones and pouty lips. I was sure that each had at least one parent that was a model. They were all too perfect.

"What the actual fuck?" I pushed my hands on my hips.

"That sounds like fun, Caleb, but I need to focus on football this year. It's senior year, time to grow the fuck up," the tallest of the guys commented as his brown eyes slid up and down my body before shaking his head.

"You're no fun, Briggs. At least Knight's with me. Right?" Caleb asked, never taking his blue gaze off me.

"You all know I am standing right here," I pointed out, tiring of being ignored.

Sure, they were genetic oddities that caused my mouth to salivate, but *I* decided who I wanted to be with, not them.

Knight shook his head. "I don't stick my dick in trailer trash."

He walked toward the school and bumped my shoulder as he strolled past, shoving his hands in his front pants pockets.

"Watch it," I snapped back.

What an asshole. I couldn't believe that was the guy who rescued me. Seraphina was right, I had wanted to thank him. Most of that night was foggy so I couldn't remember what he looked like, but now that I met him, he could go suck a bag of dicks.

He turned back to face me. My skin hummed as his gaze licked up my body. The air was electric. I did not understand why my body was acting like this around him. He practically knocked me down.

"It's you who needs to watch it." Something dark passed over his face as he said, "You don't belong here and you never will, trash."

I didn't get a chance to tell him off like I wanted because right as I opened my mouth, Seraphina pushed past me, too. Only she wasn't as gentle.

FIVE

Violet

I HELD THE ICEPACK to my lip. That damn bitch caused me to have a bloody lip.

A grand, wood-burning fireplace framed Principal Lyndon as he leaned back in his black leather chair. "This isn't a good start, Ms. Adler."

The principal's office was like something I'd expect to find in a castle. Green Hills Academy looked old and a little spooky.

"You can say that again," I mumbled into the icepack.

The chair squeaked as he sat up.

"I am serious." He pushed his thick red hair back as it fell into his eyes.

He was another overtly handsome person. Maybe it was the water? If I drank from the faucet, would I grow several inches and become hella gorgeous?

But the principal was older. Someone who would be around my father's age, if I knew who my father was. That was a tidbit my mom took to her grave.

Now I won't ever know who contributed the second half of my genetic makeup.

"You've already been in a fight before class. This doesn't look good for you."

My brows shot up. "Fight? You think this bloody lip is from a fight? Seraphina pushed me to the ground—"

He held up his hand as his cell phone went off.

Tapping at it, he smiled.

"We can discuss this another time, Ms. Adler. My daughter is here."

I nodded, thankful to get out of my morning conversation with Principal Lyndon.

The door opened and in walked a gorgeous girl with shoulder-length red hair.

"There's my girl. Violet, I would like you to meet Arabella, my daughter."

I nodded. Was she like the rest? Nice in front of adults, but then turned into a complete asshole? I suspected with a principal as her father, she had an air of protection around her. Easier for her to get out of trouble.

Ugh, first Seraphina and her bitch squad, then Knight, whose parents named him wrong because he was as far from a knight in shining armor as you could get. And his friends weren't much better.

Now I was face to face with a girl who could easily whisper in daddy's ear any lie she wanted about me.

"Nice to meet you," I gritted my teeth but forced myself to produce the phoniest smile I could.

Fake it until I got the fuck out of Green Hills. That was going to be my senior year motto.

"So, you're the new girl from South Green Hills?" The corner of her mouth ticked up.

"Yup." My shoulders felt tight. I hadn't

even started class, and I already wanted the day to end.

"Arabella, I want you to show Violet around. This is an enormous building, and she might need some help today."

Her hazel eyes slid to my lip and she nodded. "It would be a pleasure, Dad."

The way she stared, I wondered if she wanted to make the other lip swollen.

"Come on, new girl." She waved me to the door. "First, we need to find your locker."

I followed her out the door. Every room in Green Hills Academy was huge, even the front office. At my old school the front office was tiny, and you had to turn sideways to get in between the desks. And the floor was a worn green carpet that had holes.

There was nothing worn about the floor here. At Green Hills Academy, their flooring was wooden and polished to a mirror shine.

As we left the office and stepped into the main hall, extensive works of art surrounded us. It really was like walking through a castle.

"This place is creepy," I said as I looked up at the portraits of people staring down at me.

"Yes. Creepy as fuck. It's haunted, by the way."

My eyes widened. "Really?"

Arabella stopped at the bottom of the rounded staircase that led to the second floor and placed her hand on the wood-carved lion's head banister.

"Apparently, a duke from some small country in Europe was the original owner. His kink was that he liked to spend time with prostitutes." Her eyes grew as she told the story.

"Okay. Did someone die here?"

"Not one, but five. I think there may have been more. Green Hills Academy is on the top of a big hill and at the bottom is a stream."

I nodded. I couldn't help but take notice of being jerked around in the car by Seraphina this morning as she whipped the car around all the curves going up the road.

"Way back when the duke lived here, that stream used to be a large river. There's a trap in the basement of this place that goes straight down the stream. The duke would kill the prostitutes and then dump the bodies down the shoot. They'd drift down river to Happy Pond, and no one could pin the deaths on him."

Why does nothing good happen at Happy Pond? They seriously screwed up naming that thing.

"Oh my god, that's terrible. And dangerous. Is the trap still there?"

"I heard they sealed it up decades ago. I tried to go down there, but only my dad and the janitor are allowed in the basement. I wanted to see if I could find the trap. See what remains of it."

That would be cool to see if it were still there.

"This place has a lot of history. I can't say I've been in a building older than a few decades or even a castle before."

She stared at me for a moment. "Did you really try to claw Seraphina's eyes out this morning?"

"What? I never touched her. She's the one who ran into me and caused me to fall to the ground." I pointed at my lip.

Lifting the ice pack, I noticed it wasn't cold anymore. Oh well. I tossed it into the trash bin in the corner.

She gasped. “I knew it. That scag always lies. But I have to say, I’m disappointed.”

“Why?”

Arabella shrugged. “I was kinda hoping you had attempted to attack her. That bitch needs to be brought down a peg or five. Her and her plastic bitch crew should’ve been thrown into the recycling bin. It’s better for the environment.”

I laughed. “Oh man, that felt good. I don’t think I’ve laughed in a while.”

She tucked some of her red locks behind her ear. “I heard what happened at Happy Pond. I’m sorry. That sounded awful.”

And just like that, my smile was gone.

“I’m still sort of numb from it. My mom may not have been the best person all the time, but she loved me and I loved her.”

She shrugged. "I get it. My mom left my dad when I was five. I've seen her twice since she's left. I don't think being a mother was in her genes, you know?"

I liked her. She wasn't stuck-up and a jerk like the others.

I nodded. "Can I ask you something?"

"Sure, ask away."

"How come you're not with Seraphina's stuck-up crew? I don't mean you're stuck-up . . . but you're gorgeous and your dad's the principal. I would have thought you'd fit right in with them."

She threw her arm around my shoulders and guided me up the steps. "I'd tell you everything, Violet, but it would take all day. This town and especially the people here in North Green Hills, aren't always what they appear to be on the surface."

"Okay." I said.

There was more to that statement but I had just met her and it was my first day. I'd leave it for now.

We got to the top of the stairs and she took me to a hall of lockers. But these weren't the dented-up metal ones I was used to. They were made of dark wood and had a gold plaque with names on them.

"Here we are. The A's." She waved at the lockers.

"A's?"

"Yes, since your last name begins with A, this is your locker area."

I glanced around and found a locker with the name Violet Adler. It was wide and taller than me—not that I was tall like Arabella.

"So, do you go by Arabella or do you shorten it to Bella?"

The scent of lilacs arrived before she

did as she leaned on the locker next to mine.

"Oh, no. Never call me Bella or they may never find your body."

I lifted a brow as I opened the folder the principal gave me, looking for my locker code.

"Sorry." She winced. "I didn't mean like what happened to you mom. Ugh, I need to shut up now."

"It's okay. I get it. You hate the name Bella."

"You have to understand, I was teased ruthlessly when the Twilight movies were out. My whole elementary school existence was kids telling me I liked to kiss vampires."

I giggled but tried to hide it by covering my mouth.

"I know it sounds silly now, but back then it was the worst."

“Hey, my mom named me after a purple flower. Every birthday gift I got growing up was purple.”

“I’m guessing you don't like purple.”

“I’m a green kinda girl.” I punched in the code and the door popped open.

“Red for me.” She made a growling sound and clawed the air with her hand.

“Maybe you do like vampires.”

She shook her head, but I saw her smile.

“Whatever, new girl. Just put your stuff in there and then we can get you to class. We’re already late, as you can tell by no one in the hallway.”

I lifted the school handbook to place inside my locker when I saw an envelope with my name on it. I guess it’s a welcome letter they gave to all the new students.

Reaching in, I grabbed it before putting the book inside.

"Wow, you work quick, Violet. Already have a secret admirer."

The envelope was cream, thick stock with a gold edge. I slid my finger along the seam and tore it open. There was a letter inside, handwritten.

My heart pounded in my chest as I read the words. With trembling fingers, I handed it over to Arabella.

"What? What is it . . .? Oh my god." She took a breath before she read it out loud, "Roses are dead. Violets are black and blue. Watch out, little girl. I'm about to destroy you."

"Do you think it's Seraphina?" I asked, wondering if she wanted to do more than just push me to the ground.

Anabella shook her head. "No, she may be a bitch, but she's all bark and no bite. The most she'll do is start a rumor about you that you like you give hand jobs for crack or something stupid like that. This is more . . ." she trailed off and her expression had me worried.

"Who?"

"Did you piss off or even speak to Knight King today?"

"Uh, yeah. Right out front of the building when I first arrived." Based on Arabella's reaction, I might as well have told her that I punched a puppy. "He called me trash and said I didn't belong here. What was I going to do? Stand there and take that shit? It's not like I called him names."

The more I spoke, the more Arabella shook her head. It's not as if I was naïve with bullying. I had been picked on back at my old school, but they never realized I knew how to defend myself. And I was getting the impression that these rich kids were clueless, too. They'd learn soon enough.

"No, no, no. When it comes to Knight, you keep your head down and never make direct eye contact." She placed her hand on my shoulder, worry creasing her brow. "I'm serious. I like you, Violet. You aren't plastic, both physically and mentally, like a lot of the kids here. I don't want to see you dragged down by what Knight and his crew can do. He's called the devil for a reason. The only time anyone purposely interacts with Knight is if they want someone hurt."

I pushed my shoulders back as I crumpled up the paper and threw it back into my locker. "Dealing with spoiled brats that think they can push me around will be easy compared to some of the stuff I've dealt with. If Knight thinks he can scare me, he's got another thing coming. The last guy who tried to intimidate me ended up in jail."

SIX

Knight

I NARROWED MY EYES and watched the door. No Violet. Good.

I prepared for today, but not for her.

"I'm thinking we celebrate the first day of school at my place tonight. My parents are still in Japan, so we have the place to ourselves," Caleb said as he leaned back in his chair, causing the wood to creak.

Caleb, Briggs, and I had the same class for first period, art. It wasn't a serious class, and even the parents didn't care if their kids goofed off in art.

Most of the kids spent the class checking their phones.

"Sure, whatever," I added, sliding my eyes back to the front door.

When I found out my uncle wanted the girl from Happy Pond to stay with us, I thought it was a stupid publicity stunt. But what I realized yesterday, when I overheard them in the pool house, was that it was much worse.

Violet was just another of my uncle's little helpers. I was sure she was using him as much as he was using her. All that trailer trash saw in my uncle were dollar signs.

"What is with you today, bro? First

there was the way you acted in the parking lot and now it seems like you're waiting for someone. Is it Seraphina? Please tell me you both aren't back together." Briggs leaned forward on our shared round table.

I shook my head. "In her dreams. I wish she'd leave me alone. I broke up with her in June, you'd think she'd have learned that by now."

"So then what is it?" Briggs gave my shoulder a tap.

I groaned and ran my fingers through my hair.

"Okay. If I tell you this, you can't breathe a word to anyone, including your sister, Caleb. Okay?"

Briggs nodded and Caleb put up his hands. "I told you, I can keep a secret from Catlin."

Briggs snorted and shook his head. "No, you can't. It's that creepy twin thing you have going. Like you two don't even need to talk to know what the other's thinking."

Caleb sat up, his chair legs hitting the floor with a thump. "I won't say a word. And if I do, you may take Silk from me for a day."

The corner of my mouth ticked up.

I pointed at him. "A month."

His eyes grew large. "Are you fucking insane? Hell no. I'll give you two days."

Briggs gave me a wink before he added, "I don't know. That's not very long. I mean, how are we supposed to take you seriously that you won't tell your sister if you only give up that sweet, silky thing for two days? Knight's going to need at least two weeks with her."

Caleb, who never appeared uncomfortable, looked like he was about to puke. "I'll give her up for a week, and that's it."

"Only if you let Knight and I both ride her for a week."

Caleb's jaw tightened. "Fine, but I will come by at midnight on the eighth day to get her back. At fucking midnight." He pounded the table with his fist, causing the class to glance up from their phone to stare at us.

Briggs chuckled.

"I can't wait to race that thing down the mountain," I mentioned just to watch Caleb squirm in his seat.

Silk was Caleb's Bugatti. It is one of the most expensive and fastest cars on the planet, and I believed he might marry it one day the way he acted around the thing.

"Enough about Silk, this thing you've got to tell us better be good for the risk of giving up my baby."

I pointed at him. "Only if you tell your sister or anyone. Just keep your mouth shut and you can go back to giving Silk a good dicking."

"Just get on with it," Caleb grumbled as he narrowed his eyes at me.

We may mess with each other, but each one of us would have the other's back if it ever came to it. All of us have been through shit.

My eyes slid to Briggs. Some of us were still just trying to survive. But we were a tight crew and never let each other down. Our families may not care if we lived or died. Or in my case, they were too cold and six feet underground to have feelings for me. But we made our own family. Each one of these guys, while not blood related, were who I considered family.

Not that joke of an uncle I had at home.

"You guys know my uncle just let that

girl who was rescued from Happy Pond come live with us?"

"Yeah, that's weird, even for him," Caleb said.

"It is. That night was messed up. And didn't go at all how I had planned."

Briggs looked around before leaning in close. "Did you get what you needed, though?"

"Not really. That stupid mother of hers fucked it all up. Now I'm back at the beginning. I need your help."

I never wanted to bring my crew in this deep, but I had nowhere else to go. They knew the bare minimum. What I was doing wasn't safe, and I hated that I was asking them to risk themselves like this.

"I told you, Knight, I'd do anything to help you. After what you did for my mom, I won't ever forget that." Briggs reached over and gave my shoulder a squeeze.

Caleb nodded. "Yeah, bro, anything. We're here to help."

"It's the new girl. She's in on it with my uncle. I overheard their conversation when she first arrived yesterday. We need to do everything we can to get rid of her."

Caleb rubbed his hands together. "I can't wait to fuck with new flesh."

I shook my head. "This will not be like messing with incoming freshmen or some dick that hit on your girlfriends." Caleb usually had more than one girl he was banging at a time, and they all knew it. "This is going to be messy. We've got to go deep. Make sure when she leaves, she never comes back."

Both Briggs and Caleb nodded. My crew would always have my back.

"And you are?" the art teacher, Ms. Chiron, asked.

I glanced over my shoulder to discover

Violet standing there.

"It's Violet Adler. Sorry I'm late, but I'm new."

"This will be the only time tardiness is tolerated, Ms. Adler. Everyone needs to be in their seat by the time the bell rings. Is that understood? Art is as important as math and English class," Ms. Chiron said despite a few chuckles in the room.

The teacher glanced around until her eyes landed on our table. Oh, no. She was going to do it, wasn't she?

"Ms. Adler, you can go sit at Knight, Briggs, and Caleb's table. We are reflecting on our summer for an art piece we will present at the end of the month."

"Oh, fuck no," Briggs said under his breath.

I turned back and shook my head.

Caleb grinned like a deranged jester. "Calm your tits. This is perfect. We can start fucking with her. Every Monday, Wednesday, and Friday, we can sit here and torment her. The three of us against the wilted little flower."

A smile broke out of my face. "I did not understand you had such a wicked mind, Caleb. I should have had you at the pond with me."

He pointed his finger at me like a gun. "That was your first mistake. Try not to make any more. Now, shh . . . she's coming."

"Is this seat taken?" Violet asked as I caught a whiff of vanilla.

I wanted to look up, but I had to ignore her. When I laid eyes on her this morning in front of the school, I had no idea how beautiful she would be.

It was dark when I stumbled upon her at the pond, and I never got a good look. Then, in the parking lot, her golden-brown eyes struck me. I couldn't stop staring.

She wasn't like the other girls at Green Hills. She was short, curvy, like a '50s pinup. And when she smiled, that sexy-as-fuck dimple appeared on her cheek, and all I wanted to do was lick it.

But she was just pussy. That's what my cock thought. And I had pussy prettier than her before.

That's why I rarely listened to my cock.

I knew what she was deep down, despite the naïve, fish-out-of-water façade she displayed. Violet was as fake as anyone inside Green Hills Academy. Played innocent on the outside, but inside, she was as rotten as any gold-digger in this town.

None of the crew answered her.

"I guess not," she said, tossing her backpack on the table. She pulled out a chair and sat.

"As I was saying, Knight, my place, tonight. It's going to be lit. My sister's friends will be there. So much pussy to go around," Caleb said with a chuckle, pushing his hands behind his head.

"They into gang-bang stuff? I can invite the football team over," Briggs offered.

I took a quick glance over at Violet. She had her head down, searching through her backpack. As she lifted a pencil and pad of paper out, I added my thoughts about tonight's festivities.

"I don't know, man. I was thinking we could head down to Happy Pond. My dealer is down there most nights, hanging. We could go for a dip."

"Shit, I don't know. Didn't you find that disgusting dead body there? Doesn't that make the water contaminated or something?" Caleb asked.

"I know what you're doing, and it won't work," she said with irritation in her voice.

I glared at her. "You want to come?"

"No, I don't want to come. You know that's where my mom died. You know because you found me."

Her cheeks were flushed, and I couldn't help but notice her chest rising and falling rather rapidly. As much as I would enjoy popping those buttons of her blouse and see how far that flush went, I remained focused on pissing her off.

"Don't remind me. If I had known I was rescuing trash, I would have left you to die, too."

Her jaw tightened and she mumbled something.

"What was that, little girl?" I cupped my ear as my lips curled.

She went pale. The entire class turned

to stare when she stood abruptly and pushed her chair over. "I said I wish you had left me to die."

Violet glanced around, realizing everyone was staring at her. After a moment, she ran out of class.

"That worked easier than I thought," Briggs added.

I glanced toward the door. "Yes, a little too easy."

This morning in front of the school, she fought back. I expected Violet to stay and fight. Causing her to break was simple.

Maybe by the end of the week, she'd be gone.

SEVEN

Violet

The next two classes were easy compared to art class—easy because Knight and his buddies weren't in them.

I noticed as I walked down the hallway people stared and whispered to each other. It must have been from me running out of first period.

When Knight called me little girl, I snapped. He must have written that note. I knew exactly what that note meant. Roses are dead—that was my mom. He was taunting me, trying to scare me . . . and it worked.

What they said in class about the party was irritating. But then he mentioned the pond and drugs and then finally called me little girl.

I ran out of class and found the bathroom, spending the rest of first period getting myself together. No one I knew was in my next three classes—no Seraphina or Knight.

Now it was lunch and Arabella told me I could sit with her.

I walked into the dining hall but didn't see a place to stand in line to get lunch. Glancing around, I noticed Arabella in the back corner sitting by herself.

I took in the room as I made my way

to her. It looked more like a dining room in a restaurant than a cafeteria at a high school.

The tables were large and round with white tablecloths. Each table had a small glass vase containing white flowers. My eyes widened as I noticed a few kids eating off milky-colored plates with gold and navy trim. There was nothing plastic about that plate or silverware. I wondered for a moment, *Was that actual china?*

They spoiled these kids. No wonder they were petty monsters. The only one who was down-to-earth was Arabella, who had just spotted me. She smiled and waved from her table.

The room was warm, and I desperately wanted to remove the school blazer but didn't dare for fear I'd attract attention, especially from the table nearby that was filled with all the people I hoped to avoid. Seraphina sat next to Knight and all their friends.

It didn't matter if I removed the jacket or not because they noticed me at the same time as Arabella.

"Oh my god, it stinks in here. Do you guys smell that?" Seraphina yelled while staring at me.

I ignored her and kept weaving through the tables to Arabella.

"You're so right, Seraphina. It's so stinky . . . like old, rotten fish," one of her bitches whined like a baby.

"Eww. I heard if you're a skanky whore and you don't see the doctor, the festering sores on your va-jayjay can start to stink. Oh . . . hi, Violet, I totally didn't see you there." Seraphina's lips curled.

I nodded at them as my jaw tightened. She was trying her best to get to me, but I wouldn't let them. If her boyfriend had a wandering eye and it landed on me, that wasn't my problem.

As much as Knight hated me, which was obvious, he sure stared at me a great deal. That irked Seraphina, which made me not mind his gaze that much. Anything to piss off that bitch.

"I'm totally not hungry now. Thanks, Seraphina," Knight grumbled as he pushed his plate of food away.

"I'm sorry, baby." She ran her fingers up his arm as he shrugged her off. "It's just that I wanted to help Violet. She has an odor problem and should see a doctor."

Knight studied me, his expression unreadable and cold. That didn't stop my nipples from hardening as if it was his fingers, not his eyes, sliding over them.

I had to force myself to keep walking.

Let him go, Violet. He hates you.

Clearing my throat, I was a few steps from Arabella's table. Her eyes brightened and she rose from the table. But then her expression changed. Concern etched her features, and she shook her head. I turned my head to find out what was upsetting her, but then I felt it.

Something cold and wet slapped the side of my head. A cup full of juice had hit my cheek. It stung a little, but the shock caused me to gasp.

The entire cafeteria erupted in laughter. I lifted my arm. The white cuffs of my shirt that peeked out of the navy school blazer were stained red from juice.

I inhaled. It was cranberry.

Turning, I saw Seraphina with a lopsided grin. She shrugged and said, "Oopsie. It must have slipped."

My heart pounded. I wanted to run over to Seraphina and beat her until she was red, too. But I never had a chance. Someone gripped my arm, and I was being pulled toward the front door of the cafeteria. It was Arabella.

"Let's go," she said as she dragged me out the door.

"That bitch. She's going to regret doing that to me."

I was angry and while I liked Arabella,

she was preventing me from making Seraphina pay. Therefore, I wasn't too happy to be around her right now, either.

"No, she won't."

I tugged my arm from her grip once we were in the hallway and stared at her.

"So what? I should just take it? Like a good little serf."

She shook her head. "I never said that. Come. I have an extra uniform in my locker. One perk of being the principal's daughter."

When I came here today, I never expected to be accepted with open arms but the non-stop harassment was getting to me.

"Fine. But I will get Seraphina back." I stomped up the steps behind Arabella.

"I don't doubt it. I only met you today, but you definitely aren't a shrinking violet." She looked back with a wink.

We stopped by her locker and she grabbed a bag, then we headed back down the stairs. But instead of making our way to the cafeteria, we turned and headed toward the front door.

The intensity of the assault was wearing off.

"Where are we going? The cafeteria is back that way." I threw my thumb behind my shoulder.

"To my car. We're getting out of here."

I smiled. She may be my only friend here at the academy, but she was worth twenty friends right now.

Once we stepped foot outside and the valet pulled up with her sporty black sedan, I felt the weight of the morning lift from my shoulders.

Getting a break from this place was like taking a trip to Heaven. If she drove me to an auto shop where I had to eat an old vending machine baloney sandwich for lunch, it would be a hundred times better than eating off fine china at Green Hills Academy.

"I hope you like old Britney, because I do," Arabella said tapping at her console and 'Baby One More Time' pumped around me.

We joked and discussed our love of all things 90s. And before I realized it, she had pulled up to a small restaurant called *Jack's Place*.

"I never expected the northside of Green Hills had a diner like this."

We hopped out and she grabbed the bag before coming around the car.

"Oh my god, yes. It's not just a diner, Violet. It's *the* place to be if you want to be free of all the plastic people." Arabella hooked her arm with mine and guided me toward the entrance.

The front door was a metal and glass door and looked retro. And once we were inside, I might have thought they designed the rest of the place to look like something out of an old movie. Only I got the feeling it hadn't been updated since it was first established.

There was something oddly familiar about it. I shrugged. Most old diners looked like this place. It's not like I had come here before.

"Come on, we can sit here." Arabella pulled me to a corner booth. "The bathroom is in the corner. Here's a new uniform."

She tossed the bag at me as she scooted over the ripped vinyl of the red-padded seat.

It didn't take me long to change. The bathroom was as old as the rest of the diner. The mirror was faded and scratched, but I could tell there was juice all throughout my hair. Thankfully, I had brown hair, so not that obvious. I washed my face and hair as much as I could in the sink before I headed back to the dining area freshly changed. My stained clothes in the bag.

"I never expected to see a place like this

anywhere near the school," I said as I slid into the booth, tossing the bag beside me.

Arabella lifted her hand and waved two fingers at the waitress behind the bar counter. The woman nodded.

"Everyone in North Green Hills has been trying to tear down *Jack's Place* for years, but they get nowhere. I suspect that Jack is some reclusive billionaire, like a Howard Hughes character, and every time someone comes to shut him down or buy him out, they get nowhere."

I raised my brow. "I'm guessing you're a history buff."

Arabella wrinkled her nose. "I know. I'm such a nerd, but there's so many crazy things that have happened here. What's fascinating is the stuff people don't know about, like details I know on certain people's parents . . . certain kings and queens of the town."

I leaned forward and was about to ask her to tell me when the waitress arrived with two milkshakes and two plates of something with eggs on top.

"I never ordered this." I gazed up at the woman with short, gray curls.

"Arabella ordered two, so I made two." She nodded before walking back to the counter.

"Violet, this is Jack's famous peach milkshake and their biscuits and gravy sunny-side up. We don't need a menu and you really don't need to order anything else."

I shook my head. "I've been to a diner before, Arabella. I usually order pancakes or waffles, or something like that."

She reached over and placed her hand on mine. Staring into my eyes, she said, "Just taste it and then you can thank me."

She knew more about this place than I did, but I knew what I liked to eat. I shrugged and appeased her. She had been nice and helpful to me today, so why not?

I dug into the dish until the yoke

oozed. When I took a bite, my eyes closed. Damn, she was right.

I chewed, savoring the wholesome goodness before opening my eyes back up. Even if my mom never made biscuits and gravy, it somehow reminded me of her and my heart fluttered in my chest.

She shoved the milkshake in front of me. "Now take a sip."

I held up my hands and mumbled, "Can I finish what's in my mouth first?"

She groaned, "Okay, if you want to be all good-mannered and shit."

Swallowing, I smirked. "Give me that. No one threatens me with good manners."

Once I took a sip, I understood I had been wrong to question her.

"It's official, you shall be my official food person. Is there a name for that? Someone who recommends food, you know, like there's people who recommend wine."

She tapped her chin. "Like a

sommelier but for food?"

I shrugged. "I don't know what that is. I guess."

She pushed her shoulders back and nodded. "Yeah, I like that. Arabella, food sommelier."

We laughed and ate, not caring that we were late getting back to school after we left the diner.

Once we drove up to the academy after lunch and hopped out of the car, I said, "Thanks. I needed that break."

She placed her arm around my shoulders. "That's what friends are for."

EIGHT

Violet

"**THANKS FOR TAKING PITY** on me and driving me home, Arabella. Again." I hopped out of her black Genesis G80. While I was grateful for the ride, I feared many times on the way home Arabella was trying to kill us.

She was a lousy driver.

"Don't think of it as a pity ride." She leaned over to the passenger seat, pointing at my backpack I had almost forgotten to grab.

"After Seraphina stood me up on the first day and the entire rest of the week, I don't know what else to think of it as."

Seraphina had no problem taking me to school, which I was realizing might be a chance to look good for the mayor, but most likely was to get to see Knight. But getting home was a problem, as she told me Monday when she drove off, leaving me behind.

"I can take you to school, too."

"Oh god, that would be heaven. Not to have to deal with the icy silence every morning in Seraphina's car. Or when she spoke, reminding me I wasn't worth the breath she breathed and that if she had her way, they would kick me out of Green Hills for just existing."

A bemused smile appeared, and she nodded. "Now go get some rest because this was only the first week."

I groaned, "I hope I make it."

Was it worth going through this hell to get a chance at the university of my dreams? I doubted it. But then my mother's words floated through my head.

We have too much spice in our blood to dissolve into nothing.

I jutted my chin out and said, "I'm sure Monday will be better."

"Let's hope. What happened at lunch today made the juice in the face from Monday look like nothing."

Hitching my backpack on my shoulder, I closed the door and waved. I watched Arabella curve around the fountain as she headed toward the street. Sighing, I turned to hide in the pool house all weekend and hoped to never run into the mayor or his nephew.

Arabella was right. Once I got home on

Monday, I showered and collapsed into bed. I didn't even wake up to have dinner that night; I was so exhausted.

Tuesday wasn't much better. Then on Wednesday, Knight and his crew still made disgusting jokes in art class, but I ignored them. Seraphina and her Bitch Crew, which Arabella had nicknamed, took any chance they could to trip me or put things in my hair. I hadn't found out until I got home and looked in a mirror that they had stuck gum in my hair on Thursday. I had to cut some of my hair away just to get it out.

As for the rest of the school, they were in on the taunting. I was the school punching bag. I lost count of how many times I'd been called trash or a whore. Some even flicked wads of wet paper at me.

But today, Seraphina tricked me. She was unusually sweet and kind, even complimenting my makeup on the drive to school this morning.

When I got to lunch, she asked if I wanted a cupcake as it was her friend's birthday. I saw they were all eating the cupcakes, so I agreed to have one. Only something was in it. I ran to the bathroom a half hour later and had diarrhea. I still didn't feel great and was afraid to eat anything.

Arabella said she must have put a laxative in my cupcake.

I went around the house to the gate and made my way to the backyard. Looking up at the big house, I wondered what it looked like on the inside. I had yet to be invited inside. Based on the mayor and his wife's reaction to me, I bet I'd never get a glimpse inside their world.

The one lucky thing about my stay here.

I heard voices inside the pool house as I reached for the doorknob. Pressing my ear to the door, I couldn't make out what was being said but the voices were deep and male.

I pushed open the door and threw my stuff onto the table by the front door.

"Hello?" I called out.

"Violet. Come in the living room. There are some people I want you to meet," the mayor said.

I had been lucky. The past several days I hadn't seen him or his wife.

My luck just ran out.

Pushing my shoulders back, I braced myself and hoped he wouldn't try anything in front of his friends. He was the mayor, after all.

I turned the corner and saw a glass decanter half-filled with dark amber liquid, which had to be scotch or brandy, in the middle of the glass coffee table. Something only rich folks drank.

Then I noticed the men, three of them. Ties askew, tumblers dangling from their fingertips, some of the amber liquid swirling in their glasses.

They all had smiles, and not the kind that portrayed happiness and welcome. No. Their curled lips told me one thing—they wanted to have fun and I was their entertainment.

The mayor waved me over to the leather chair with the wide arm rest where he sat.

"Come, Violet. Sit here. This is John Lenker and David Sherer. You two must meet Violet. Isn't she beautiful?" I stepped closer, but nowhere near the mayor or any of those men. I kept myself close to the entrance of the room in case I needed to escape.

The name Lenker sounded familiar. I wondered if he owned the Lenker tractor company. Probably.

"You were right about her, Ichabod. She is gorgeous," one of men said as he stared at my legs.

"When they're young like that, John,

they're so soft," the mayor added.

"It looks like you three are busy, I'm just going to my room now—" I took a few steps back and was almost out of the room when the mayor hopped up.

He was by my side before I had the chance to get away.

"What's the rush?" He slid his arm around my back and his fingers curled around my upper arm. I winced as they dug into my skin and was pulled farther into the room.

Both John's and David's eyes sparkled from the alcohol and their smiles grew when the mayor placed me in front of them.

"She's shy. We might have to take our time with her." Ichabod chuckled.

Bile rose in my throat as I noticed one of the men already had a hard-on tenting his pants. He had white hair, bald on top, a pot-belly, and looked to be about as old as my grandfather when my grandfather was still alive.

"I got all night." He sat up and reached over to touch my thigh.

I slapped it away. "I'm not a prostitute. I'm seventeen."

Creep.

He didn't even acknowledge me.

"She's feisty. I like it."

"Now, Violet, remember when I asked you to do some things for me when you first came? Well . . .." He waved toward the men.

My mouth fell open.

"Are you serious? You're pimping me out to your sleazy friends?"

He shook his head. "These are men I've worked with when I was on the board of *Franklin First*."

I wouldn't care if they were on the Nobel Peace Prize board and were considering me for the top honor. There would be no way I'd do anything with them.

I tried to pull away, but the mayor had a stronger grip than I had anticipated.

"We're old friends."

"You got the old part right," I sneered.

The mayor's fingers tightened until I yelped from the pain. He reached up and grabbed my ponytail, yanking my face to his.

"Listen here, you little brat. You are going to do what I say or there will be consequences. And trust me when I say . . . I know lots of people. Lots of important people who can make your life hell."

I cleared my throat and then spit in his face. Fuck him. It's one thing to be a little handsy and creepy when I first arrived. But making me get fucked by his skeezy old friends was so far from okay, I'd need a telescope to find it.

That's when I felt something hit me in my stomach. I doubled over and fell to the floor. For a moment I thought I would throw up, but nothing came—probably because I already shit everything out earlier in the day.

Wrapping my arms around my stomach, I gasped for breath. The nausea came in waves and I wondered if I could ever stand upright again.

I felt something press down on my legs. Glazing over, I saw the mayor straddling me.

"If you're going to be such a little bitch about it, I think I should be the first to go. Cristen that teenage pussy." He nodded toward the men. "David, grab her arms. I can't get any scratch marks on my face."

I held my arms firm and desperately wiggled my body, but David was strong, too. They may be old and fat, but they had some strength to them.

That's when I realized I had a voice. I opened my mouth and tried to scream, but nothing came out. My heart pounded in my chest and I put all my strength into saying something. I didn't know if it was the punch to my stomach or just plain fear that wouldn't let me yell for help.

I closed my eyes and wondered, was this it? The moment I lost my virginity would be from being raped by these old assholes.

Hot tears streamed down my temples as I tried to gain traction with my feet, but his weight kept me pinned in place. Even as my arms were held down and I watched the mayor try to frantically unzip his pants, I fought.

He was to take care of me, not use me.

If one of them got close enough, I'd use my teeth if I had to.

My hips pushed and swayed as I struggled with little success to push him off me. That's when my voice came back.

I opened my mouth wide and screamed as loud as I could.

"Stuff something into her mouth. Get her to shut the fuck up."

I had never stopped yelling for help.

Even as the one guy who wasn't holding me down tried to stuff something that reeked of sweat into my mouth, I kept it up.

He made the mistake of pushing the cloth in with his finger and I chomped down.

"Ow, you fucking bitch!" he yelled.

As I pushed the stinky gag out of my mouth, there was a flash of pain across the side of my face. One man hit me. I hadn't been paying attention, too focused on getting rid of the gag to notice who it was, but it hurt. Light flashed in my right eye as the sting on my cheek throbbed.

"It's time to make this bitch pay," John said as he reached for my shirt and ripped it open. Tiny mother-of-pearl buttons flew everywhere.

My anger gave way to fear as I felt fingers grasp my upper thighs and pinch my nipples. Nothing about this was sexual or delicate. These men wanted to hurt me.

They enjoyed exuding power and watching the fear in my eyes.

I was their prey, and they had won the prize.

NINE

Knight

The sun was warm on the early September afternoon. When I arrived home from school, I lounged by the pool and did a little spying on our new guest.

Violet.

It had been a breeze messing with

Violet over the past five days. It was like playing keep-away with a toddler. I got a thrill watching her cheeks flush and those pouty lips stiffen.

She broke so easily on Monday in art class that I thought she had no fight left. I was wrong. But it made it all the more fun.

As I sat on the lounge chair ready to pull off my T-shirt to soak in the last rays of the year, I heard someone yell.

Pulling my shirt back down, I cocked my head and noticed it was coming from the pool house.

The screams grew louder, and I realized it was Violet and she was screaming for help.

I hopped up and grabbed my cell off the iron and glass side table. I groaned, hoping the klutz hadn't fallen over and hurt herself.

Opening the door to the pool house, I froze. The screaming had died down, but I heard my uncle. He was telling someone to muzzle her.

The hair on the back of my neck stood up as I knew what he was doing. It's not as if this would be the first time I had walked in on my uncle fucking someone who had no interest in him.

I remember the relieved and grateful look on the woman's face as I stood in the pantry doorway my uncle thought he had secured. And how could I forget the angry stiffness of my uncle's jaw as he yelled at me to leave.

When I first arrived at his home two years ago, that's exactly what I did. I was young and had recently lost both my parents when their private plane took a nosedive into the Atlantic Ocean.

My uncle frightened me, and with my little sister here, I wanted nothing to happen to her. I went along with turning a blind eye, but my eighteenth birthday was in three weeks. If I wanted, I could leave and take my sister with me.

He doesn't scare me anymore.

I lifted my phone and turned on the camera to record. Walking down the hall, I heard her scream again.

My heart rattled in my chest, but I put on the practiced face that my uncle had grown to hate. I pretended to be bored as I turned the corner and zoomed in on each of the men's faces before filming Violet.

One man slapped her hard enough for me to hear it at the entranceway. My jaw stiffened, but I remained focused on what I was about to do.

My hands shook as I had an intense urge to hop over the couch and rip them off her before beating them until they bled.

It was time for this to end.

"Oh, please, don't let me interrupt you," I drawled. "I'd hate to stop three men way past their prime resorting to rape because that's the only way they can get it up."

The two men, who looked familiar but I couldn't place, gasped and scrambled back.

Violet immediately spit out what was in her mouth and pushed up. Once she was on her feet, she ran around the couch and out of the room. Not once did she look at me. I saw no relief in her eyes, just anger.

As for my uncle, he smirked as he stood and fixed his pants.

"You can put the phone down, Knight, I know you're only bluffing. I'm your uncle. We're family."

See, that right there was why I hated the fucker. What a hypocrite. Hearing him go on endlessly about how Green Hills needed him to watch over them. As if he was the father of the town. The kids he vowed to care for were afraid of what he would do to them.

"That's funny, I thought the only thing you cared about was your wallet and your dick." I smirked but lowered my phone. "I mean, that is why my sister and I are here, isn't it? You want to siphon off her inheritance before she turns eighteen."

It was too late for me. I was weeks away from turning eighteen but it's not like he didn't try to *adopt* me in the past two years.

As if I'd let that disgusting pig be my father.

"Look around you, Knight, I don't need money. I have millions."

The two men's eyes bounced back and forth between us and I wondered if I called out, "boo!" to them, they'd run off as if I was about to haunt them.

"Millions, huh?" I rubbed my chin and took a step closer to my uncle. "Sounds so small, doesn't it? Because I'll have *billions*."

It didn't take long before one man tried his best to suck up to me. They were just as pathetic as my uncle.

"I never wanted to be here today. Ichabod has bribed me since—"

"Shut up, John," my uncle bit out as he

glared at the man.

My shoulders shook as I chuckled. "My, how easily they turn on you when they realize who has the money."

My uncle remained silent as I swiveled on my heels, about to leave the room.

"Knight, your sister is only six. It's going to be a long time until she gets to leave this house. I suggest you play nice with the man who's watching over her . . . at night." My shoulders tightened.

I stood ready to lash back at him but decided now wasn't the time. Let him think he was still in control. It wouldn't be long before his pretty façade crumbled into dust.

"I'll play nice," I grumbled as I left the room and continued down the hall to Violet's room.

There were only two bedrooms in this place, so it wouldn't take me long to find her.

She was in the larger bedroom, which

made sense. Bigger was better.

I knocked and got the response I had expected.

"Go away before I stab you."

I smirked. Violet was a wild animal trapped in a gilded cage. It might be a pleasant diversion to tame her.

"You're such a tease. Is that the come-on line you use in the trailer park?"

After a few seconds, the door swung open and a breeze of vanilla brushed my cheeks. She had changed out of her ripped uniform and that ponytail was gone; her long auburn hair was tousled, cascading down over her shoulders. I liked it.

"You just stood there and filmed it like a sick fuck. What the hell is wrong with you?" Violet stood there with fire in her eyes and the heat was directed at me.

As my gaze drifted down her body, I took in the perfect fit of her jeans. Her T-shirt was old and worn, the blue lettering of Nirvana was peeling in spots, the fabric knotted at her hip frayed slightly.

I leaned against the door frame. "I pictured you more of a BTS sort of girl."

She rolled her eyes and turned back toward her bed. A suitcase lay open with clothes haphazardly thrown in.

"The shirt's my mom's." Violet picked up some clothes, rolled them into a ball, and threw them into the case.

"So you don't like the band?"

Her eyes fluttered up toward me for a moment before she shrugged and went back to tossing clothes around.

"I never said that. I like them, I guess. I grew up listening to that classic stuff."

"Grunge. It's called grunge. If you listen to it, you should at least know the music you are listening to."

"Okay, professor." She jerked her hip and rested her hand on it. "You going to stand there and give me a history lesson in music or are you going to apologize?"

My head went back as laughter

rumbled out.

"I don't see what's funny. I could have been raped." She stopped packing and crossed her arms over her chest. For a girl who tried to pretend nothing affected her—as I had witnessed over the past several days—she wasn't doing a very good job right now.

"It's you who should be thanking me. I saved you, again."

She glared at me, but I wouldn't budge.

"Right. If I remember correctly, you regretted the first time and wished you had left me for dead."

"Still do."

The muscle in her jaw flexed. "What the fuck is your problem? I have done nothing to you. I haven't done anything to anyone in this whole spoiled petty part of the world. Yet everyone seems to hate me and takes any chance they can to try to destroy me."

For a second, I could relate to her. But

I shook my head and focused on what mattered.

"Because we here in North Green Hills find you and your kind repugnant. You are useless to society. The government always has to spend money on you people, yet all you do is complain that you have it so bad. You say we're spoiled, but it seems to me the people where you're from are the spoiled ones. Take your mother for instance—"

She marched over to me and slapped me across the face before I could finish. I rubbed the stinging spot and grinned.

"Need some sugar with that spice?"

"You shut your mouth about my mom. You never knew her."

With pink cheeks and wide eyes, she glared up at me. Her tits rising and falling as the anger for me, for my uncle, for the world she'd never be a part of, affected her more than she wanted to admit.

"I know she died of drugs. A single,

drug-addicted mom from a trailer park. How more cliché can you get?"

She brought her hand back, but this time I grabbed her wrist before she could strike me.

She tried to twist her arm away, but I held firm. With each tug, it pulled something in me. I wanted to reach around and draw her closer.

"Get the fuck off me."

She fought, but it wasn't much. It was all show. Her gaze avoided mine. Was she afraid of what I would discover in her eyes?

"Why do you pretend when I know you want me."

"You're so full of it. Rich, spoiled, and conceited. Nice combo, asshat."

Yet her gaze remained on the ground.

"And you're trailer trash. You can take the trash out of the trailer park, but you can't take the dirty whore out of the cunt."

She smirked and finally looked up.

"Aww, you must have mommy issues, too. You jealous of your uncle because he got to me first?"

God, she had a smart mouth, and all I wanted to do was shove my tongue inside it. Did she realize that's what I enjoyed most? The hunt.

My nose flared as I stared at what I wanted.

"Those lips would look real nice wrapped around my cock."

Her tongue darted in and sucked in her bottom lip.

I wanted to fuck her but now wasn't the time. My uncle screwed with her head by messing with her body today. She needed time to process. I wasn't like my uncle or any dip-shit who stuck their cock in a pussy just because it was there.

I let go of her wrist and ran my fingers through my hair. Taking a deep breath, I got my cock under control.

"You leaving?" I nodded toward the

suitcase.

"That's the plan. No way I'm staying here with the rapey mayor stopping by anytime he wants."

"You got a place to go?"

She frowned and scratched her arm. "My aunt isn't returning until the end of the month. I'm sure a neighbor has a spare key to let me inside."

I nodded. "Can you get to school during the day?"

There was just something about Violet. I came here to make sure she left, but now I was wondering if she might come in handy.

If she was helping my uncle before, he ruined it today by pinning her down. She might help me instead.

"It might take a few bus rides, but I'll get there."

I grabbed her hand and pulled her toward the door.

She yanked back and stopped. "Where

are you taking me?"

I reached for her hand again and this time, she followed.

It wasn't until we went inside the main house that I finally answered her.

"I'm taking you to my room."

TEN

Violet

I TURNED IN EVERY direction, taking in Knight's bedroom. It was amazing.

"Surprised?" He stood by the doorway, watching me with amusement.

"Yeah. I expected to find posters of people being tortured and severed fingers floating in formaldehyde-filled glass jars."

"Funny, feisty, and a comic."

The ceiling was vaulted and on the opposite end of the room was a large glass door that led to a balcony. But the bed was the best part. It was huge and typical dark gray and blue because he's a guy, but it was on a platform. And right above the head of the bed was a waterfall encased in glass.

"Sorry to disappoint you, but I'm not a serial killer." Knight walked over toward his bed.

I shook my head. "I never thought serial killer but potential mob boss maybe."

Taking a break from all the opulence, I glanced over at him and noticed a tiny smile. Sexy dimples appeared. I held back a groan.

He wasn't a nice guy, even if he had stopped his uncle and those creepy guys.

Sure, he could have immediately yelled at them to not rape me instead of film it, but he ended up stopping it.

Maybe he hated his uncle like I did. He lived with him longer than me. I couldn't imagine the shit he had seen or heard from that man.

"My dad was a scientist, not a mobster."

"But I heard you tell your uncle you're a billionaire. I may not know any scientists, but I don't think they make that much money."

Knight rubbed the back of his neck. "My mom. She was a Saget."

"*The* Sagets? The family that made its money in oil and land back in the nineteenth century?"

He nodded.

"No wonder your mom married a man with the last name King. You're American royalty."

"Whatever." The way he was fidgeting with the lighter he picked up on his bedside table, I suspected he didn't want to discuss his parents.

I guess we had that in common. Talking about my mom with these spoiled brats was like giving myself a hundred slashes with a knife and then taking a dip in the ocean.

"Why am I here?"

It was best to get to the point and get out. I still had some packing to do. The sun was setting and if I wanted to catch a bus, I didn't want to do that in the dark.

"Your mom died, remember? And then my uncle thought you'd be a fun toy to keep in the pool house."

I swallowed. Just thinking of what happened to me in that place made my skin crawl. I felt nauseous. I never wanted to step foot in that pool house again. But I had to grab my stuff.

"I meant in your room."

He tossed the lighter down and sat on his bed, patting the spot next to him.

"Oh, hell no." I moved toward his door.

Why did I agree to go to his room? He was probably just like his uncle; a teenage version of the mayor. Instead of ruling the town, he ruled the school. Knight King was the devil.

Right as I made it to the entrance of his bedroom, Knight jumped in front of me and held his hands up.

"You need to learn to listen," he said, holding onto the frame and blocking my exit.

I pushed against his chest, but it was like trying to move granite.

"And you need to learn to read the room. Girl who almost was gang raped," I pointed at my head, "not really interested in sitting on a boy's bed."

His head went side to side. "You have a point. Perhaps we should do this in Ava's room."

"Your sister?"

He nodded. "She usually is watching cartoons now, so she won't pay attention much to what I have to say."

I raised an eyebrow and took a step back. "Will she pay attention with what you do . . . with me?"

His gaze darkened and he lowered his arms to his sides. "I would do nothing like what my uncle did to you or anyone. I heard my nickname before, the devil . . . but even the devil had standards."

"I see."

He shook his head. "No, you don't see." He took a step forward until my tits rubbed his abs. "Pathetic animals do shit like what my uncle did. And if I hear about my sister seeing or even hearing anything that might upset her, they are dead."

His words were laced with a darkness even I was afraid to question. He loved his sister, that was obvious—and that alone made me wonder if the devil's heart wasn't all black.

I cleared my throat and said, "Then take me to your sister's room."

He stepped out into the hallway and I followed. We passed several closed doors before we arrived at one with a purple and black wreath wrapped in tulle and fake black birds clustered at the bottom.

"How old is your sister?" I stared at the wreath in surprise.

"Ava's six."

"Oh. It's just the wreath is rather dark for a six-year-old girl."

He shrugged as he pushed open the door. "She likes Disney movies."

That didn't explain the macabre wreath.

"Okay." I peeked inside, wondering if I was going to find a mini Wednesday Addams.

What I found was another vast room. A four-poster bed with a canopy of purple and blue lace hanging down. There were strings of twinkly lights all over the ceiling. The floor was a dark hardwood with a bright purple rug in the middle.

Small furniture filled the room. A white desk and chair were near the bed. On the opposite side of the room was a purple couch with white and blue fluffy throw pillows. A huge doll house was on a table near a large window and a little girl stood in front playing with the figures inside.

"The princess can only wake from a true love's kiss," she said.

"Ava," Knight called to her sister in a gentle tone.

She turned, her long, dark braid flinging over her shoulder, and her round blue eyes widened. She may have black hair and a taste for dark colors, but she was no Wednesday Addams. When she smiled, as she had at the sight of her brother, the dimples in her cheeks deepened and she reminded me of a cherub.

"Dopey!" she yelled and ran over to Knight, throwing her small arms around his neck as he knelt to meet her.

"Dopey?" I questioned with a chuckle.

Knight ignored me. He pulled back from Ava and planted a kiss on her cheek. "Hey, Ava, I have a new friend. She's going to be staying with us for a while."

What? I never agreed to that. Last I checked, I was packing to run as far as I could from these freaky fuckers.

Ava blinked and turned her head to me. She had the same stern expression her brother usually sported.

"Hi, I'm Ava. And who are you?"

I waved. "I'm Violet."

Her face exploded in happiness. "Like the purple flower?"

I nodded.

"You are beautiful and must be a princess. That means I'm your evil overlord. I'll feed you, but you won't be happy. You'll only want to escape. And at some point, you must clean my room." She pointed at me with a stern expression.

I rolled my lips over my teeth and nodded. Wanting to be evil must be in their genes.

"Ava, she's a guest. We won't make her clean your room."

Ava frowned and folded her arms. "You're no fun, Dopey. All I want to be is an evil stepmother one day. I finally have a real life princess right in my room and you won't let me live my dream. Why can't I be Maleficent?"

Ah, now I understood the color scheme and the love of Disney movies. She didn't want to be a Disney princess . . . she wanted to be a Disney villain.

I stepped forward and sat on the floor next to Knight and Ava. Holding out my wrist, I said, "Do you see this?"

"Yeah, it's a gold bracelet with charms."

I smirked. If it had been genuine gold, my mom would have sold it for drugs and not given it to me on my birthday.

"No, it's a princess bracelet. And anyone who steals it becomes my overlord." I watched Ava's eyes light up with delight, so I continued, "But I won't take it off for anyone. Only when I sleep do I remove it."

I had watched enough princess cartoons when I was little to understand what captivated an evil villain wannabe.

"She can stay in the room next to mine." She grabbed my hand and pulled me before I got up.

I stumbled to my feet and we made our way to a large bookcase.

"Watch this." She reached for a dark brown leather book and pulled. The case popped open. It was a secret door.

Because of course, it was.

"Wow, that's cool."

She pulled it open and waved for me to follow. Of course, I was going with her. When would I ever get a chance to go through a secret door again?

I thought it would lead to the next room over, but it didn't. Inside the bookshelf door was a narrow passage. There were wooden 2x4s and insulation lining the walls. Though only a small amount of light came from her room, I saw the floor was plywood. We were walking between the rooms.

We moved to the end and I thought that was it. There was nowhere to turn but Ava reached up, hopping up and down, and I noticed she was trying to grab a string.

"Here, let me." I reached up and got it.

"Pull it down," she told me.

I did, and a section of the ceiling fell open with a creak. A folded-up ladder was sitting inside. She waved me back and pulled the ladder straight.

We both climbed up to an attic. Not much was in it except for some toys and books that must have been brought up from Ava.

"I come here sometimes. My brother tells me when I hear my uncle coming, I should come here. It's my fortress."

My heart sank. I remembered hiding from one of my mom's exes—only I didn't have a fortress to protect me.

There was still innocence in her sparkling eyes, but for how much longer?

Anger snaked up my spine and entangled my heart. If the mayor wanted to try something with me, at least I had a chance of fighting back, but Ava was only six.

I tightened my fists by my side. He was a monster, and he held this little girl hostage.

I heard movement from somewhere in the darker part of the attic. Where Ava and I stood there was a small bit of light streaming in from a window on the wall far above. I had no idea how big the area was, but that window seemed to be the only light source.

Stepping in front of Ava, I looked around for something to fight with. Unfortunately, I was surrounded with plastic toys that didn't look strong enough to do any damage.

"Who's there?" I barked out.

I gasped as I heard his voice.

ELEVEN

Violet

I REACHED AROUND TO make sure Ava was safe and stayed behind me.

"Just the serial killer." Knight emerged into our small, light-filled section of the attic.

"How did you get in here?" I glanced

behind us, wondering how he got up that ladder and around us without me knowing.

He threw his thumb behind him. "From your room. There are multiple entrances to this place."

"My room?"

Ava tugged on my hand again. I followed and darkness fell. My eyes adjusted, but it was hard to make out what was in front of me.

I felt a much bigger hand slip into mine. "Watch your step." Knight's hot breath slipped down my neck. Electricity tickled my arm as the heat from his body slid over mine. He must only be an inch from me, but I only saw darkness.

He guided me to another opening and ladder on the floor. Once I was down, I glanced up as he told Ava she needed to head back to her room. I waved goodbye to the interesting and adorable little girl.

Knight came down and we walked

through another insulation-filled passageway until he pushed on a spot in the middle of the wall. It opened, and inside was a bedroom.

There was another bed on a platform, but it looked like the opposite of Knight's. A pale pink, button-tufted, upholstered headboard with white and pink linen and pillows.

A round, faux-fur rug encircled the bed, at least I thought it was faux-fur. Near us was a matching upholstered chair. Once we stepped inside and closed the door, I realized why the chair was there. It was another trick bookcase. This area was made to look like a cozy reading area.

"Wow, are all the bedrooms amazing?"

"That doesn't really matter to me," Knight said as he ran his hand through his hair.

I stepped around him and walked farther into the room. It was gorgeous.

"Why did you say this was my room? I

told you, I'm leaving."

He shoved his hands into his swim shorts pockets. "Because if you want to stay safe, I suggest you not run away."

My brows went up. "Are you for real? You told me on Monday that I didn't belong here. That I was trailer trash."

"You don't belong here, but my uncle dragged you here for some reason. And if you run off, he'll assume you're going to the authorities or worse, social media. He'll realize that his career would be in jeopardy and do everything in his power to destroy you."

Fuck. Everything Knight was saying was right. From the first moment I met the mayor, he threatened me. Who's going to believe the word of a girl from nowhere who's mom died of drugs over the mayor?

I rubbed my brow and went over and sat on the edge of the bed. Damn, the bed was soft. I hated that everything—minus the people—was amazing and luxurious. I wanted to enjoy the opulence, not be fearful of getting too comfortable.

"My aunt," I said in a whisper.

"You have an aunt? Why isn't she taking care of you?" He came over to the bed and pointed to the opposite edge to sit. It was far enough that I felt much more comfortable than sitting right next to him.

"She travels for her work and wouldn't really be around to take care of me." I shrugged. "I turn eighteen in two weeks, so it's not that it matters. But getting to go to Green Hills Academy would help my chances at getting into Winter River University."

Knight narrowed his eyes, studying me for a moment. "Who told you about Winter River?"

"My mom." I tucked some hair behind my ear. "She went off some years ago when she was still using. I thought she was crazy, making up a story about how elite it was, but when I looked it up, I discovered she was right. It's sort of been my obsession ever since to get in."

Knight tapped his chin. "And let me guess . . . my uncle threatened that if you didn't play nice, he'd make sure you never got in."

I frowned. "Yes."

There was silence for a moment.

"Why are you being so nice to me?"

Knight leaned back on his elbow and looked up to me. "You don't belong here."

I groaned, "Yes, you've said that like a million times."

"No, what I meant was . . . you don't belong here, yet here you are. Why? I don't trust my uncle, but that's because of personal reasons. But that doesn't mean he's not up to something that's larger than me and my family."

I flopped back on the bed but kept my eyes on Knight. God, it was amazing. Even the bed in the pool house wasn't this nice.

"I thought he was just taking me in for

his image. You know, politics. Some do-gooder shit to get him re-elected."

Knight laughed. "Yes. I thought about that, too. But then I realized it was never just about his image. There's always something else there that he wants. That he wants you to live with him means he has you here to monitor you. That you know something that could hurt him."

"I know he tried to rape me."

"Long before that."

Suddenly, I felt exhausted and rubbed my face. "I only met him for the first time when you found me at Happy Pond. The night my . . . my mom died. And he never said a word to me."

"Huh. Nothing before that? Did your mother ever mention him?"

I yawned and shook my head. "No. And I doubt my mom knew him. I really don't think your uncle ran in the same circles as my mom had."

It was a struggle to keep my eyes open.

What Knight was telling was true. The mayor was the real villain but Knight was his family. For a lot of people, blood was thicker than water. Or in the mayor's case, blood was thicker than image.

Maybe Knight was lying to me too.

As much as I fought it I closed my eyes just to rest for a moment. Except it wasn't a moment later when I opened my eyes.

I must have fallen asleep because it was dark and I discovered a warm blanket over top of me.

As the fogginess of sleep cleared, I wondered how I was going to get out of here. Throwing the blanket off, I hopped out of bed. I was about to turn toward the door when a twinkling light caught my eye.

It was coming from the window. The room was rather high up and overlooked the pool. The moonlight must have bounced off the pool.

I was about to leave when I noticed a

light on in the pool house. I didn't remember turning on any lights as it was the afternoon when I was last in there.

Then I saw movement. A dark shadow passed across a window in the pool house. My heart went still. *Who was that?*

A thought came to me, but I didn't want it to be true. Was it the mayor coming back for me?

The light went out and a moment later, the front door to the pool house opened. Instinctively, I stepped behind the curtain so if he looked up, he wouldn't see me.

I peeked around until I got a good look of who was coming out. I gasped when I saw him.

It wasn't the mayor, but it was his nephew. Was Knight going back to get some of my things?

I didn't see my luggage on him, but he was holding something. I squinted to get a better look.

They were objects. I think one was a

vase that was in the bedroom I was using in the pool house. But I couldn't make out what the other thing was because right as I leaned toward the window, Knight looked right up to my window.

I hopped back, hoping he hadn't seen me. My hands were shaking.

Nothing about Knight made sense. He was mean to me all week long. Art class had been terrible, and I asked the teacher if I could move but she explained once seating was assigned, it couldn't be changed. Which was a load of crap.

Knight and his buddies constantly discussed who they would fuck or have fucked and asked if I wanted to be on their to-be-fucked list. Or they'd make lewd jokes and bring up my mom every chance they could get.

I had grown more accustomed to their disgusting behavior and even the comments about my mom. Knight got the entire school in on teasing me. I couldn't walk the hallways without being called trash, whore, or people telling me how I should have drowned with my scum mother.

After an entire week of that, he'd suddenly looked out for me? I couldn't believe a guy who had the nickname the devil and enjoyed bullying me would instantly change his mind about me just because I was almost raped.

Maybe it was a good thing I was staying in the house now. I would have access to his room. Then I might find out why he wanted to take care of me.

TWELVE

Violet

"**When you asked me** to take you to school early today, I thought you wanted to study, not break into the guy's locker room." Arabella's eyebrows moved up as we strolled down the quiet hallway toward the gym.

It was Monday, and the only person I saw all weekend in the house was Ava. She kept trying to take my bracelet from me, which was amusing.

I had heard from the cook that the mayor was going to be gone for the month, taking a holiday in the Mediterranean. I felt relief and joy all at once of the news that I asked if I could be the one who made the pancakes. The cook was surprised but let me. Ava loved my chocolate chip and strawberry pancakes.

Not only was the mayor not around, but neither was his wife. As for Knight, he was around but rarely came out of his room and when he came out, he locked his door.

The sexy jerk must have known I would snoop.

"It's not like that. I want to find Knight's gym locker."

She grabbed my arm, stopping me. "Whoa there, newbie. I thought I made it quite clear that you avoid Knight at all costs. He's the devil."

I nibbled my bottom lip wondering if I should tell her. Part of me was hesitant because I didn't want my only friend possibly getting hurt. She might want to help, and then she'd be involved. What if the mayor went after her, too?

But I felt alone for so long. My friends from my old school had yet to reach out to me. And when I texted them several times, there was no response.

"If he's the devil like you said, then I think he has his eyes set on me."

"Duh." She laughed and rolled her eyes. "I thought it was obvious given how he treated you last week."

I shook my head. "No, I mean something more than just making school life difficult. He told me on Friday he didn't want me to leave."

Arabella's eyes widened. She pulled me behind a set of lockers and lowered her voice. "When exactly did he say that to you?"

It was now or never.

"Something happened when you dropped me off on Friday. Something involving the mayor and his friends. And let's just say what he did to me was the opposite of treating a guest with respect."

"Violet. Did he hurt you? Did Mr. King do something that we need to go to the police about?"

I bit my bottom lip and nodded. Then I went and explained exactly what the mayor and his buddies did to me on Friday but stopped short telling her how Knight walked in on us.

She wrapped her arms around me and for the first time since before my mother died, I felt comfort and warmth. Arabella hugged me and whispered, "There's a rumor about the mayor and I didn't know if it was true."

I pulled back. "What?"

"He only ran for mayor because he wanted a way to control the police so no one found out about his . . . fondness of young girls."

My hand covered my mouth. I felt sick and Ava instantly flashed in my head. No wonder Knight told her to hide in the attic if she heard the mayor coming.

I closed my eyes as hot tears brewed. "Shit."

"Did he, you know . . ." Arabella trailed off.

"No. That's the thing. Knight showed up right in time and then took me into the house."

She tilted her head. "What do you mean, took you in the house? You are already living there."

"I stayed in the pool house and wasn't allowed in the main house."

"Ugh, the more I hear about the mayor, the more I think he needs to stop being re-elected and thrown into jail.

What he did to you was wrong and you need to get out of that house. Stay with me if you have to."

It was tempting and I wanted to say yes so badly, but then my thoughts would drift to Ava. She may not be my sister, but I understood what it was like to live in the home with a monster at that age.

"I can't. The mayor may be disgusting, but there's more to that sleezy-rapey dirt bag than you think. That's why Knight wants me to stay. He thinks the mayor may go after me if I run. And since he owns the police, he easily could."

Arabella took a step back. "Fuck. That is messed up. Okay." She rubbed her forehead. "Okay, we'll work with what we have."

"We? No." Placing my hand on her shoulder, I shook my head. "It's me. I don't want to risk you or anyone else. Keep this to yourself, okay?"

"Violet, he's obviously dangerous, and

from what I know about Knight, he's not much better."

"Maybe if I find out why Knight wants me in his house, then I can figure out . . ." I trailed off as a thought wormed its way into my head, and it involved my mom's death.

"What? Why he's such an asshole? I can tell you why."

"He's rich, handsome, and a future billionaire. Of course, he's an asshole," I said before she could.

Arabella shook her head. "That's not the reason. He got his nickname two years ago when his parents died. Think about it. He had the best parents in the world; I know, my dad complains all the time about some of the parents here. I know who has shitty parents and who doesn't."

"Your dad liked the Kings?"

She made a 'hmm' sound before she said, "I guess so. I don't really remember, but I used to be friends with Knight. And

Seraphina, if you can believe that."

My mouth fell open.

"No freaking way. Why? I mean, how? I mean, why and how?"

"It was different when we first came here. We were all so innocent." She sighed. "Ahh, the youthful years."

"What changed?"

"Anger, hormones, tragedy. Knight lost his parents. Briggs mom remarried and his new stepdad is a beast. While I don't know this for sure, I have a feeling Caleb's parents don't exactly do things by the book. Why they had kids, I'll never know. They aren't the most loving people."

I nodded. Tragedy and tough times could change people, I knew that all too well.

"As for Seraphina, I don't know what's her problem. She became obsessed with Knight as a sophomore and turned into the shallowest bitch I have ever met."

"I guess Knight used to be a nice guy?"

"Yeah, it's too bad he turned into such a jerk. But just because he was nice years ago doesn't mean he won't fuck you up if he catches you going through his things."

"Maybe you're right." My eyes slid over to the end of the hallway, to the front door of the boys' locker room. "I guess since I'm here, I'll head to the library and get some studying in before school starts and all the kids arrive."

I hated lying to my friend, but the less she knew, the better. The devil was playing a part; that much I knew. Why else would he pivot so quickly from making my life a nightmare to helping me? He needed me for something, and I had to discover what that was.

This was my life being toyed with, not Arabella's. I wasn't about to rope her into my problems.

"Okay. Well, I'm going to the gym and check out the cheerleader try-outs."

My head went back in surprise. "You

want to be a cheerleader?"

"Oh, god, no." She snort-laughed. "There's some people in school, myself included, that like to taunt the cheerleaders. It's like a rite of passage. If they can't hack it, then they have no business being a cheerleader."

There was a dark side to Arabella.

"So, just the cheerleaders?"

She waved her hands out in the air. "No. We do all the team tryouts, sports and otherwise. Football, basketball, soccer, lacrosse, and the chess team."

I held back a laugh. "Okay, seems harsh, but I get it."

I waved bye to her and moved down the hallway away from the gym. Once I got to the end, I waited until I saw her enter the gym. Then I turned around and headed back. The entrance to the boys' locker room was on the left of the gym entrance, right next to the girls.

I glanced around and saw no one was

around, so I opened the door. Peaking inside, I lowered my voice and yelled out, "Hey."

There was no response.

My heart thundered between my ears as I scurried inside. Glancing around, I was happy when I discovered the lockers were exactly the same as the girls' locker room, which were mini versions of the lockers in the hallway—and that included the name on each locker.

All I had to do was find Knight's locker. I kept going down the first row. Nothing. Then the second row. Again, no sign of King.

Finally, the last row in the middle was the one I was looking for. I almost squealed in glee, but my excitement was short-lived.

There was a padlock on it. The only locker in the gym changing room with a lock.

Since the girl's lockers had no locks, I

assumed it was like that in the boys. I never thought Knight would bring in his own.

I pounded my fist on the locker. Dammit.

I was so close. Maybe there was a way to get the key from him for the lock. An idea popped into my head that made me smile.

Looked like I needed to play a game of princess and the evil queen once I got home.

THIRTEEN

Violet

"**What are you so** happy about? These back to school rallies are mind-numbingly dumb. Their only purpose is to re-establish the pecking order and give the popular kids a chance to suck their own dicks. *Oh, God, I'm so great. Yeah, that's* *it, please, tell me how wonderful I am.*" Arabella made many gestures with her hand as if she was sucking a dick.

I couldn't help but laugh, especially as more people turned to glance our way.

Even stares from the students couldn't stop the smile on my face. I got the key to Knight's gym locker from the help of his sister. That girl was clever and from what I had witnessed, could manipulate her brother into almost anything.

"Oh, look. Arabella is doing a reenactment of how Violet begs for food from the mayor," Seraphina called back to us before her bitches started cackling.

I narrowed my eyes at her. Why did she mention the mayor? Did Knight tell her what had happened?

"That's funny because I thought she was showing me how you begged your plastic surgeon to make your tits look like two rhino asses putting on sweaters for the winter."

She gasped.

"You have no idea who I am, do you?" she said in her best spoiled-brat voice.

I groaned, "Yes, you won't shut up about it. 'Look at me, I'm balloon-tittied Seraphina, with the crystal headlights and bubble-gum brain. One day I hope to marry a senator and turn a blind eye when he pays to fuck whores because doing me is worse than nails on a chalkboard.'"

Arabella belted out with laughter, as did most of the surrounding people.

"You're such a bitch. It's sad you try so hard with Knight when I'm the one fucking him."

My jaw tightened. I shouldn't care who Knight was fucking, but something about it made me angry.

"You two are perfect for each other. The devil and his ankle bitch."

"Ankle bitch?" She snorted. "Oh, Violet, I think you've done too many drugs. You've lost it. That means nothing."

She was sitting two rows down from me and to my right, so I leaned closer. "Oh, that's right, you never went to my school in South Green Hills. An ankle bitch is someone who clings to a man's ankles, taking whatever scraps he cares to give. Then licking his dirty feet because that's as close as she'll ever get."

"Damn," Arabella yelled before exploding into more laughter.

"You're a cunt and after this rally, you'll be the laughingstock of the school, trash!" Seraphina bit out before turning back around and having her bitches console her wounded, spoiled heart.

"It's fist-bump time." Arabella held out her fist. "That was epic and worth sitting through a hundred boring rallies to witness."

I gave her what she wanted and chuckled. Seraphina needed to be put in her place.

"Has no one ever told her off before?"

"Oh, no. She's the queen of the school. And her father own half the town, so technically, most of the people here either work for her dad or have property her dad had sold them. Her father owns a bus line and that organic and natural foods grocery store chain, *Earthy Foods*. It's like he has his hand dipped in every pot you could imagine. And her mom is the social queen bee of the town. Because her parents are so powerful, the people don't dare knock Serphina."

"I guess you're the only good person at this school."

"I'm not perfect." Her eyes slid over to where Knight and his friends were sitting, close to Seraphina.

I wonder what was going on there.

I didn't have time to ask as the rally started. The principal came to the middle of the gym and announced various upcoming events.

Arabella and I kept talking and ignored

what was going on until I heard the words Winter River University.

"What did he just say?" I asked.

"My dad's talking about the senior fall field trip. It's just to a local college."

I had never heard of a school taking a field trip to a university before.

"Did he say Winter River?"

Arabella nodded. "Yeah, the seniors take a trip there every year. I mean, since the Kings founded the university back in the seventeen-hundreds, they always invite Green Hills Academy to Winter River University."

My fingers touched my parted lips.

"I thought it was Knight's mother's family who had all the money."

She leaned closer. "The Sagets, sure. But they didn't become wealthy until the last half of the eighteen-hundreds. It's the Kings who descended from French royalty. A cousin of King Louis XV of France came here before the

Revolutionary War and bought up a bunch of land. Brought the castle over from Europe, stone by stone."

"What don't you know?" I giggled.

"New girl, I know everything." She waved her hands around the bleachers. "It's a benefit to being the principal's daughter and resident history nerd."

"There are lots of perks with that. You think your dad would adopt me?"

The room darkened and a hush came over the room.

"The film teacher made this over the summer. The Green Hills Academy history. A short film about the founding of the school," the principal announced.

I nudged Arabella with my shoulder. "Did you help with this?"

"No, and I'm kinda pissed Ms. Brill would take me out for coffee and use my brilliant mind like that, but then take all the credit."

We chuckled as the film began. The

production was high quality, but the acting was high school drama club level.

We were in the middle of laughing about the telephone wires clearly on display in the background of a scene that took place two centuries ago when the film stopped—as if it had been purposely edited that way and a dark and grainy film took over.

I narrowed my eyes to see what was happening. The location seemed familiar. That's when it hit me.

That's my bedroom in the pool house.

"What the fuck," I mumbled.

Arabella leaned over and whispered in my ear, "Is that you?"

"Y-Yes." My throat dried up as I barely got the word out.

My ears burned and I couldn't take my eyes off the screen. It was me getting undressed in my bedroom. The camera was angled from above, coming from somewhere on the ceiling.

In the footage, I had my shorts off and was about to take off my top when the chanting started.

"Take it off. Take it off," the students yelled and as if on cue, I did just that.

I lifted my hands to my face. Grateful I was wearing a bra on screen, but I knew what was coming. That bra would not stay on for long. I didn't want to see what came next.

Someone had done this. Someone had filmed me. And the only someone who had access to that pool house and went to Green Hills was Knight.

I lowered my hands and scanned the bleachers for him. He was gone.

Everyone had their gaze hypnotized to what was on the screen, except for one person. Seraphina.

She winked at me and mouthed, "Whore."

I gritted my teeth and got up. There was no way I would stick around to continue to be humiliated.

I stumbled down the steps with voices continuing to yell around me.

"Nice tits, trash."

"I got five bucks; will you strip for me?" I kept my head down, racing down, and then scurrying toward the gym door.

Once I was out in the hallway, I inhaled. It had felt like I was suffocating in there.

I slumped, leaning against the wall. Looking around, I was thankful I was alone out here.

I had started the day with a newfound energy. Ava had played along with my game of finding the secret key to get my bracelet, which was just my way of getting her to tell me where her brother's gym key was hidden.

It wasn't a deception I was proud of. Tricking a little girl for something wasn't who I was. But I had to find out why Knight wanted me around.

I turned my head. The boys' locker room door was right there, and everyone was in the gym.

While they laughed at my privacy being violated, I would violate the privacy of the person responsible. That put a smile on my face.

I made my way to the boys' locker room door. Opening, I yelled in with no response.

Once inside, all I could hear was the muffled boos from the gym. Someone must have stopped the video. I shook my head when I noticed they didn't stop it until I was nude.

When I walked to the back and found Knight's locker, I dug into my jacket pocket and held up the tiny silver key.

I was about to unlock the door when I heard the gym door creak open. Slipping the key back into my pocket, I dashed toward the showers. Slipping inside one of the showers, I closed the curtain and waited.

"That dumb bitch."

My brows shot up in surprise. I had expected to hear a boy's voice, but I heard a girl. A very specific girl. Seraphina.

There was a clicking noise and then she said, "I'm calling you because I told you to keep a lookout at the door."

There was a pause before she continued, "I don't care if Briggs wanted to talk to you. You keep watch or I'll tell everyone about your abortion."

I covered my mouth.

"Oh, boo fucking hoo. I don't care if your dad made you. Maybe that will teach you not to sleep with the help. Now shut up and keep watch."

Seraphina stopped talking and the creak of the door to the boys' gym door let me know someone else was coming.

"Hey, baby," Seraphina said in her nauseating baby voice.

"Seraphina, what are you doing here?"

Knight asked.

Shit. I took a step back and wondered if I'd ever get out of the shower.

"Surprise! I thought we could get undressed and I could suck you off in the shower."

I knew it. Ankle bitch.

"God damn, Seraphina, get off me. How many times do I need to tell you it's over? We broke up in June. Get the fuck over yourself."

"Baby. I know you want to be free for senior year, but that doesn't mean we can't fuck. Besides, you owe me."

What? I tilted my head closer to the curtain.

"That's sad. Just pathetic. You have to bribe someone to fuck you."

I sucked my lips over my teeth to stop myself from laughing. What I would give to be recording this right now.

"No, what's sad is you drooling like a lost dog all over that trailer trash. It's pathetic, Knight. You know she's just using you and your uncle to go here. I wouldn't be surprised if she drugged her mom just so all this could happen."

My jaw tightened. I wanted to pull the curtain back and pounce on that bitch.

"The deal is going to be done in two weeks. After that, I'll give you what you want, okay, Seraphina? But not today."

"Fine. But you better live up to your promise or I'm telling everyone. No more pushing me away."

I heard someone walking and the door opened. I stayed silent in case both hadn't left. But the locker room was quiet. After a minute, I risked it.

Pushing open the curtain, I peeked my head out.

No one was there.

Stepping out, I slipped between the locker rows and as I turned to the last one, I came to a stop.

Knight stood there, leaning against his

locker, and said, “I knew you were a lot of things, Violet, but a snoop wasn’t one of them.”

He got up and walked toward me, and I backed up. Knight didn’t stop. His jaw tight, his brow furrowed, I understood why everyone called him the devil.

Hair lifted on my neck. He reached toward me with his hand; I tried to pull back, but I hit the wall. I was trapped.

Sweat beaded at my temple as heat traveled down my body.

Knight grabbed my jaw, pushing my face up toward his.

“I hate being spied on. And since you can’t seem to keep yourself out of trouble around here, I guess I’m going to have to teach you a lesson.”

FOURTEEN

Knight

Her lips were wet. I could barely concentrate as I stared at them. Savage thoughts tore through my mind. I loosened my grip and slid my hand down her fragile neck.

"Fuck you, Knight. Is this what you get

off on? Pushing people around? You love being an asshole."

I squared my shoulders, my gaze never leaving her mouth. Violet took one look at me on day one and decided who I was. To her, I was spoiled and wealthy. Someone to be hated or used and cast aside. She probably learned that from her mother.

The bitch got under my skin. I wanted to torment Violet, cause her to cry. But my cock was rock-hard and begging for her lips.

I never mixed with trash.

My eyes slid down until I watched her tits rise and fall. They had to be natural, and that was a pleasant break from all the fake ones I had touched lately.

Why say never? Maybe I could torture her and get off at the same time. I smirked, wondering if she tasted as wicked as her tongue.

"But you like that, don't you?" I took a step closer until my body pressed up against her. "What was that term you used? Ankle bitch. That's your big secret. You want to be my ankle bitch." I slid my hand down until I cupped her tit.

She sucked in a breath through her teeth. Her eyelids fluttered as my thumb traced around her hardening nipple.

Violet bit her lip. I knew she had to be wet. Just watching her pretend I wasn't what she needed had me grinning.

"You tell me to stop anytime you want, Violet."

Her hands moved to my chest and for a moment, I thought she might push me away. But they kept going until she slid her fingers around my neck and pulled me onto her lips.

They were as sweet and soft as I imagined. Had I yanked my cock to her imagining those lips? Hell yes.

But reality was a thousand times better. I inhaled her sweet scent, and her taste was just as decadent. Our kiss was hard, needy, and I never wanted it to stop.

I wasn't like this for any girl. It was as if my cock and my heart were battling over a game I hadn't realized I was playing.

My arm tightened, pulling her in, rubbing her over my hard-on. My lips meandered down her neck.

"I'm going to taste you."

"What?" she said breathlessly.

I lowered to my knees and slid my fingers up her thighs. Her brown eyes grew.

"Do you want me to stop?"

My finger trailed up her thigh, under her skirt until I was tracing her panty seam. As I thought, she was soaked.

Violet pressed her thumbnail to her lower lip and shook her head. "No." She reached down and slid up her skirt like curtains rising for a spectacular show.

For someone with so much attitude, she wore the most innocent panties—light pink cotton. I was about to drool all over them.

Instead, I slid them off and tucked them into my back pocket.

"Here, hitch your leg up on my shoulder." I grabbed her thigh and adjusted her over me.

I savored the moment. Her small patch of dark curls framed pink, glistening lips. She smelled like everything I loved in the opposite sex. So sweet and spicy, and I bet she tasted delicious.

I edged closer until my tongue slid over her. She inhaled, her thighs tightening, and her hand moved my head back.

"Someone might come," she said with worry wrinkling on her brow.

My lips curled. I wondered if she was more innocent than she led on.

"I know someone will come." I curled my lips, looking up at her. She wasn't having any of it. "Nobody spies on me, remember?"

She smirked. "I did."

"And that's why you're being punished."

I slapped her ass cheek and she yelped. I watched her as my fingers slid over her lips and around her clit. It wasn't long before she was rotating her hips, wanting more.

I loved to work girls up until they begged. It made me so hard. But with Violet, I suspected she'd easily melt into a puddle.

Slipping one finger inside, I fucked her as my thumb played with her clit. She easily surrendered to my touch.

My nose flared. God, she was sexy. She began unbuttoning her top until her tits fell out.

I reached up and pulled back her matching pale cotton bra cup. Her cute little pink nipples were like pebbles. I pinched and pulled.

"Oh, fuck," she whined.

Violet was so wet my hand was soaked.

I had to taste her. Lowering my head, I slid my tongue over her clit and slipped another finger inside.

Her fingers curled into my hair, pulling me closer. She was grinding on my face.

My tongue darted out to give this dirty girl what she wanted. A teasing swipe and then another. Her fingers dug into my hair harder. She was hot, needy, and I drank it all in.

She didn't understand why I was on my knees in front of her. If she did, I doubt she'd still be in the locker room. But I needed Violet, and I hadn't realized until my uncle pinned her down in the pool house.

Why not enjoy myself a little as I used her?

I felt her tense and I knew it wouldn't be long before she came. I hadn't planned to fuck her, but my cock ached to be inside her. It deserved a little thank you for waiting so patiently.

Her back arched and she ground out my name. I groaned as if she was already riding me. Hearing her cry out my name was all that I needed.

I jumped up and held her. Violet wobbled in my grip. Her eyelids fluttered open and I smiled. She was dazed and heat bolted to my cock, knowing I did that to her.

Flipping her around, I bent her over, pressing her face against the wall.

"We'll make this quick. The rally won't last much longer."

And neither would I.

"Yes," she said. "But I need to—"

We both fell silent as we heard the door to the locker room open. Damn. I was looking forward to sinking my cock deep inside her pussy. But that was going to have to wait for another day.

Pushing down her skirt, she turned. I

pressed my finger to my lips to make sure she knew to be quiet. Violet mouthed the word, "Obviously," before rolling her eyes.

Even post-climax she was a smartass.

I pulled her along the wall toward the back by the showers. She was about to turn into one shower, but I shook my head.

I had a better place to hide.

Waving her back, there was a door marked Do Not Enter. Most people ignored the door, but I went exploring one day about a year ago. It was locked, but that had never stopped me before.

Taking the chain from around my neck, there was a cross. I wasn't particularly religious, but no one here ever questioned why I wore it. They probably assumed I found God after my parents died. Whoever they were had no idea what I really found.

"Are you about to pick a lock with a cross?" Violet whispered.

"I like to think God wanted me to break

into places I'm not allowed."

"You're the worst," Violet said with a small smile.

I concentrated on the lock until I got the last pin. Opening the door, I said with a wave of my hand, "It turns you on, doesn't it?"

She shook her head as she moved into the darkened room.

Once we were inside, I closed the door as gently as I could. Switching on the light, it was a hallway and at the end were a set of stairs leading down.

"What is this place?" She moved toward the stairs.

"It leads to the basement."

Her eyes rounded and she came to a stop.

"You mean the basement with the shoot that leads to the river?"

"What? What shoot?"

She grabbed my hand and pulled me to the steps. We found another light and made our way down. As we did, she explained the history of the place and that at one time there was a hole in the basement floor that led down into the river.

She looked around the vast expanse of the basement. Parts were dark and broken up with walls.

"We need to find that shoot," she said glancing around.

Violet was turning out to be much more useful to me than I thought.

My lips curled. "Yes, we really do."

FIFTEEN

Violet

"I KNOW THE RALLY was tough today, but by the end of the week most everyone will have forgotten about it," Arabella said laying on her purple velvet chaise lounge.

I sat in the white leather chair, which was shaped like an egg, and pushed my foot on the floor, causing it to spin.

We were in her room and should be studying but had yet to crack open our laptops.

"Says the girl who wasn't being filmed naked in her bedroom for the entire school to see."

Arabella's lips curled. "Who ever said I hadn't been filmed naked in my bedroom?"

"Oh my god, you whore. Tell me all about it." I stopped the leather egg chair and smirked.

She held up her finger. "First, they filmed it on my camera, so I have the evidence, not the other guys."

"Guys? As in plural?"

She studied her fingernail as if our conversation was the most boring thing in the world.

"It's my thing. Look at me, Violet." She

waved her hand down her body. "There isn't a boy in all of Green Hills that could satisfy all this. I require *several.*"

I tilted my head. "How exactly does that work? Do you, ya know . . ." I waved toward my thighs. "Do them one at a time or all at once?"

"You're cute, Violet. You do whatever you want with as many as you want." She winked and we laughed.

"So how about you? What's your kink?"

I bit my lip, wondering if I should tell her. While she was the only friend I had at Green Hills, I had only known her a few weeks.

"I don't know?" I answered with a shrug.

"What do you mean, you don't know? Wait, oh no . . . don't tell me the guys you were with didn't know what they were doing? That's the problem with high school boys." She shook her head. "I'd be surprised if they lasted longer than thirty seconds."

Heat traveled up my neck. "It's not that. It's because . . . I'm a virgin."

That caused her to sit up.

"Shut up. I didn't realize there were still virgins that were eighteen. Not that there's anything wrong with that. I too was a virgin once."

I wasn't about to inform her that my eighteenth birthday was still days away. She'd want to celebrate it and I wasn't a celebrating sort of girl.

I shook my head. "Everyone was a virgin once, Arabella."

"You know what I mean. Have you done nothing?"

"I've done stuff. Just today Knight and I—" I stopped myself before I let it out.

She jumped up and ran over to me,

taking a seat at my feet on the floor. "Knight? The guy nicknamed the devil? You did what with him?"

Shit. I hadn't meant to tell her any of this. It's not like my virginity embarrassed me. But there hadn't ever been a guy I wanted to go all the way with. That was until the locker room with Knight.

What he did with his lips and hands was like nothing I had ever experienced before. I was so lost in the high of my orgasm that I didn't care I was giving it up to the boy who called me trash.

"Please don't tell anyone."

She looked around. "Who? Who would I tell? My dog, Mittens? Yeah, she's like best friends with every dog she comes in contact with, but she'd never let it slip."

I giggled, lightly slapping her shoulder. "I'm serious. It just sort of happened. It's weird. He's been terrible to me and called me trash. I hate him with every fiber of my being but... I can't stop thinking about him. You know?"

She nodded and I pushed my shoulders back to prepare for explaining the hottest experience of my life.

"It's totally normal. It's a hate fuck and it's the best."

My eye's widened. Just the thought of having sex with Knight was soaking my undies.

I took a fortifying breath and said, "So, when I ran out of the rally, I hid in the boys' locker room."

She waved her hand in the air. "Waiting until after you tell me the good bits before I ask why you were in the *boys'* locker room."

"Anyway, Seraphina showed up, so I hid. I think she was breaking into Knight's locker, but then he showed up. They got into a fight, so she left. I thought he had left too, so I came out and there he was. He must have known I was there because it was like he was waiting for me. He was angry and pushed me against the wall."

"Okay, here we go. The good stuff." Arabella rubbed her hands together.

"It was the way he was touching me. Rough but not too rough. I couldn't help it. When we kissed, a part of me wanted to push him away. My mind kept screaming at me to get out of there. But that's not what my body was telling me."

"And that's your kink. See, everyone has a kink. You like it a little rough."

I bit my lip and kept going. "He fell to his knees and—"

She gasped. "I knew it. It's always the guys who act like jerks that love to eat pussy. Was he good?"

I didn't even get to answer her.

"I'm guessing by that mega-blush that he's phenomenal."

I grabbed her hand. "That's not the most important part. I mean, it was amazing . . . and I had never come that hard ever, but something happened after that I wanted to tell you about."

She sat back on the floor, looking deflated. "Oh no, don't tell me he's tiny." She waved her pinky finger at me. "Maybe that's why he's such an asshole. He is making up for his itty-bitty pencil dick."

I snorted. "Stop making me laugh, I'm being serious. No, I never saw his . . . *you know.*"

"Oh, God, you are a virgin. It's called a cock. Or, if you want to be a little more formal, a penis."

"Anyway, someone walked into the locker room, so Knight and I ran to the back to hide. I was going to hide in one of the showers, but he went to a locked door and picked the lock."

"Wow, never realized he knew how to pick locks. Why pick them when you can pay others to do it for you?"

"I know, I was shocked too, but guess where that door led?"

She rubbed her earlobe. "I don't know. His evil lair?"

"The basement."

Her mouth fell open. She sat there for a moment, not saying a word. Then she hopped up to her feet and grabbed me, pulling me with her.

"You know what this means, Violet? We need to find that trapdoor."

"I tried looking, but it was dark and there's a lot of old furniture down there. It would take a while to find it. Knight and I weren't down there long. We both had to get to our next class."

"Okay." She started walking in circles around her room. "We need a plan. Pick a time when no one is around and go there."

"I think Knight wants to find it, too."

She came to a stop and glanced over at me. "I'm sure what he did to your nether region was spectacular. He could probably suck the sugar out of an apple with those lips, but he's the devil, Violet. There's no way I'm going into an old, dark basement with him. That's b-horror movie shit."

I nibbled on my lip. She was right. It was strange how eager he was to find that hole in the floor.

He wanted to help me, and then suddenly, he was interested in the basement. Nothing about him made any sense.

"There's a party at Happy Pond Saturday night. Most of the school will be there. We can go to be seen and then after a bit, we'll leave and head to the school. That way we know the school will be closed and no one will stop by. It's a Saturday night. Who would be there?"

That was a good plan, except for one problem.

"There's no way I'm going to Happy Pond."

She frowned and came over, placing her hands on my arms. "I can't imagine how hard it is for you to even think about that place, but it will get us witnesses. Lots of witnesses. If someone sees some shadowy figures breaking into the school, there's no way they could say it was us. We could point to the party."

"It is a good plan, I'm not saying it isn't, but I really can't go there."

She sighed, pulling me in for a hug. "How about we hang out in the parking lot? That's usually where they have the kegs. Tons of people there, too."

I nodded. "Okay, but only the parking lot."

She pulled back from the embrace and pat my head. "That's my good little criminal."

SIXTEEN

Violet

"**COME ON. PICK UP**," I said to myself.

I sat at the King's marble countertop bar in their massive French country-style kitchen, picking at a granola bar half out of its wrapper.

My aunt's voice came on, asking me to

leave a message as she couldn't get to her phone.

"Hi, Aunt Dahlia. It's me again. Just wondering where you are. Haven't heard from you in a few days and since it's my birthday . . . I-I kind of wanted to hear your voice."

I hadn't been able to get a hold of my aunt for several days and I was starting to worry. That wasn't like her to never get back to me.

"Birthday!" a sweet voice yelped from behind.

I ended the call and turned in the cream leather bar chair.

"Hi, Ava. How was school today?"

The mayor hadn't been back since the pool house gang rape incident, and I was wondering if it scared him. *Good.* Once I figured out what was going on with Knight, I was going to turn my claws on the mayor.

She waved her hand at me. "Never mind about school. Let's talk cake. What have you ordered and how many layers?"

I snorted as she shimmied over in her little brown uniform. She was adorable. I wanted to lift her up and squeeze her.

"I'm guessing you like cake." I held out my hand, helping her up to the bar chair next to mine.

"Doesn't everyone? My favorite is red velvet with that cream cheese frosting." She clutched her heart and pretended she was about to faint.

The girl was too much.

Knight walked in the kitchen. His gaze flickered to my mouth. I sucked in a breath as the memory of yesterday in the locker room looped in my head.

He was across the room, but the hairs on my arm pricked as if his fingers were skating across my skin.

"Dopey! It's Violet's birthday. We need to have a party."

His brow arched and he strolled over to lean against the counter, right next to me. Heat radiated off him so intently, I felt sweat bead on my brow.

"We should. We will pull out all the stops. Balloons, streamers, a pinata, and cake."

"Don't tell me you're into cake, too?" I glanced up at him, trying not to stare at his mouth.

"What can I say . . .? I love to *lick* the icing."

That caused my eyes to fall straight to his lips. How could I not? They were full, seductive, said dirty things, and knew how to make me scream. I may not trust the guy, but that didn't mean he wasn't hot as fuck.

Ava's clapping shook me out of my dirty thoughts and back to reality.

"Look, I don't really make a big deal of my birthday . . .." I put my hands up to stop their planning. "Usually, it was me and my aunt watching Disney movies and eating takeout. Nothing fancy."

I felt a small hand grip my arm. "You don't have cake on your birthday? That doesn't make sense."

She pursed her lips, and I could tell that cute, little brain of hers was trying to calculate how a person could technically have a birthday without cake.

"I don't get it either, Ava. But you know what? She's our guest. Maybe we should surprise her." A devious twinkle lit Knight's gaze.

I held up my hands. "I appreciate the gesture but really, I don't want to make a big deal of it. Not to be a downer, but knowing my mom isn't here to see me turn eighteen makes me just want to hang out in my bedroom. Alone."

I hopped off the stool and waved at them. My mom usually forgot it was my birthday, that's why I always hung out with Aunt Dahlia. But there was something about knowing she was gone and would never come back—instead of just out getting high—that felt like there was hole deep inside that would never be filled.

Last year was the first time she remembered. I twisted the key charm of the bracelet she gave me as a gift for my sixteenth birthday.

Once I got upstairs and opened the door to my room, I threw off my Green Hills Academy jacket and went straight into the attached bathroom. It seemed every bedroom had en-suite bathrooms.

The shower was longer than I usually

took. My insides were at war. I didn't trust Knight, but every time I was around him, I wanted him to kiss me exactly like he had in the locker room. I couldn't forget the awful things he had said about me and to my face, but that didn't stop his filthy words from exciting me down to my very core.

What made it even worse today was that most of my thoughts weren't about him or the plan to break into the school basement on Saturday night. They were about my mom.

It devastated me she wasn't here. Something felt unsettled whenever I thought about her. I kept remembering when they pulled her out of the pond.

And then it came to me today as Arabella dropped me off after school. I watched the fountain out front of the King's house as I got out of the car and thought how much my mom hated fountains. Anything involving large amounts of water. She had a fear of drowning.

I wondered if it wasn't paranoia but some type of sixth sense. Or maybe I just missed her.

I stepped out of the shower and wiped some of the condensation from the mirror. There were dark circles under my eyes.

Getting enough sleep this past week had been sporadic. All the crazy, dark shit I had experienced over the past five months felt like it was seeping into my body and tearing me down a little day by day.

I lifted my nose into the air and took a sniff. I smelled pizza.

Throwing on my old, worn jammies with little pink hearts, I opened the door.

Once the steam cleared, I saw balloons. Lots of them. All were blue, green, and of course, purple.

I suspected Ava had a say in them.

"Surprise," both Ava and Knight sprang out from the corner.

My hands flew over my heart and a huge grin broke out on my face.

"What on f— earth?" I almost said fuck but realized that wouldn't be appropriate in front of Ava.

"It's your surprise party. I know you said you wanted to be alone, but you need to be happy. As your overlord—"

I held up my wrist, showing off my bracelet.

"*Almost* overlord." She rolled her eyes and folded her arms over her chest. "It's my duty to make sure you eat cake on your birthday and are happy."

I got my bracelet back as I was tiring of

her demanding that I clean up her room.

I scratched my head. "But that sounds like something a fairy godmother would do."

She waved me off and sashayed like the diva she would grow up to be. "I think I know more about being an overlord then you do."

"Let's get on with the party. Okay, Ava?" Knight asked.

"Yes. That's what I've been hoping to do, but she's fighting me. If anything, blame her." Ava stopped her pacing in front of Knight and pointed to me with her hip jutted out.

"Blame me for what?" I said, half laughing.

Knight shook his head. "Don't get her started."

Living in the same house with these two, I knew I would not be left alone.

Might as well accept my fate.

"So, where's the cake?" I strolled over to my bed and sat.

Ava held up a little bell and rang it. My bedroom door opened, and one servant rolled in a serving tray, like the kind they had in hotels.

He parked it in the middle of the room and left, but never closed the door. Then another tray rolled in a few moments later. It had two large pizza boxes and plates with silverware.

"We didn't know what type of takeout you liked, so we decided on pizza."

I nodded. "Smart choice. I don't know of anyone who dislikes pizza."

My eyes slid over to Knight, who was picking Ava up and swinging her around. They were laughing. I had never seen this side of Knight before. It surprised me he could be, well . . . nice. Sweet.

It was understandable that he would be that way to his sister. But then there's me. Recently he hated me, and now he's throwing me a surprise birthday party?

I wanted to question it. Ask him why he was doing all this. But I was tired of fighting. It felt like I had been fighting someone all my life. My mother, teachers, boyfriends, the mayor, and kids at school. Yeah, Knight was on that list too, but maybe I didn't have to fight him anymore.

Perhaps he was just being nice because we got to know each other a bit. And when he saw me almost raped, something had changed in him in how he treated me.

If he could change, then maybe I could, too—or at least, just for today. It was my birthday, and damnit, I was going to enjoy it.

Knight pressed a button on the wall by my bed and the painting across the room slid down with a large screen television emerging in its place.

"I had no idea that was there."

He turned to look over at me and smiled. "There are lots of things you don't know about this place."

The way he said it made me wonder . . . perhaps, I should keep fighting him.

SEVENTEEN

Violet

IT WAS DARK. THE sky, glittering diamonds on a sea of black velvet.

I let out a breath and watched it cloud the air. It was too much like that awful night. I wanted to leave.

Arabella's arm swung around my

shoulder. "We aren't near the pond. It's a good five to ten-minute walk down the path to get to the pond. We're safe here."

Car lights flickered in my eyes as they found parking spots.

"I know you're right, but my heart feels like it's about to run for cover."

Nothing looked familiar, but I guess I never spent a lot of time in the parking lot of Happy Pond back in April.

"All we're going to do is walk around the parking lot a few times. Make sure some people see us, then it's back into the car and we head to the safety of the Green Hills Academy basement."

My eyes slid to hers. "That sounds *so* much better. A dark old basement at night. Yeah, I'm not scared at all."

"Hey, we got each other's back. If the ghost of the butler that died in the library with a candlestick comes after you, I'll jump him."

"That sounds an awful lot like the

boardgame, Clue." I laughed and shook my head. "You're the most ridiculous person I've ever met."

"Ridiculous and sexy." She winked.

We strolled around the lot and went up to a few people to ask where the keg was located. One asked if we heard about Shawna Lenker's dad disappearing. Arabella informed me she was a member of Seraphina's bitch crew.

I felt bad for her. Even if she was a bitch and chose bitchy friends, I knew what it felt like to worry. To not know where your parents were.

We went and filled a cup. Neither of us were going to drink it because we wanted to be as sober as possible for our endeavor. But I was eying my drink, wondering if I might need some liquid courage.

"I called it, ladies. Total lesbians," a shrill voice called from behind.

We turned to discover Seraphina and her bitch posse with one less bitch in tow.

I guess Shawna took the night off.

"Wow, Seraphina, what a putdown." Arabella stepped forward, waving her hands around. "Oh, wait. No, it's not because it's the twenty-first century."

I covered my mouth with my hand, holding back my grin.

Seraphina narrowed her eyes at Arabella. "It doesn't matter, everyone knows you're a slut. Banging the lacrosse team."

Arabella chuckled. "And? You act like that's a bad thing. Oh, no. That can only mean one thing . . . you've never been fucked right. No wonder you're such a bitch all the time." Arabella frowned mockingly. "I'm sorry."

One of the bitch crew members snorted but stopped when Seraphina's head whipped around and glared at her.

"You two deserve each other. The slut and the trash heap," Seraphina added before turning to leave.

"Now that was a fist-bump moment," I said walking up to Arabella and tapping her fist.

"You inspired me, new girl. I figured if you could come to a new school after all that's happened to you and stand up to Cruella de Bitchface, then I could, too." She glanced off across the parking lot and narrowed her eyes.

"I think it's been enough time here. Maybe we should head to our location." I gave her an exaggerated wink.

"Hold that thought. I see something I need to take care of and then we can head out." Arabella walked away before I had time to stop her.

One of the reasons I agreed to show up here was that she would be at my side the entire time. I was never the shy girl or had to cling to a friend at parties, but being back at the location where my mom died left me feeling rather jittery.

"Didn't expect to find you here."

Knight's voice came from behind me.

I turned to find him with his friends.

"I didn't really want to come but Arabella . . ." I trailed off throwing my thumb over my shoulder.

"Knight, we're heading down to the pond. You coming?" Briggs asked while checking his phone.

Caleb kept staring at my chest with a smile. He had never really been mean to me, but the way he was staring made me uneasy. I folded my arms and covered my chest.

"Oh, don't cover it up. I thought you liked them hard." He lifted his hand up to cup his mouth, as if he was whispering a secret to me. "It makes them easier to tug. Isn't that what you like? The rough tit play."

My eyes widened. I had been a little chilly since I got here, but now I was burning up.

"What the fuck?" I glared at Knight.

"You're an asshole."

I pushed Knight as I plowed past him. I didn't know where I was heading. All I wanted was to get as far away from Knight as possible.

Were all the boys here disgusting assholes? I guess teenage hormones and full bank accounts meant you could treat people like toys.

As I weaved through the cars, I headed toward the edge of the parking lot that led to the woods. I marched on the grass, ready to hide in the trees. Wondering if I should just build a tree house and live amongst the creatures, away from the cruel humans.

A hand grabbed my arm and pulled me back. It was Knight. I tried to yank back but he his grip was tight.

"Violet, don't run."

"Why? You don't like to have to work for your prey?"

"They're my friends. Yes, I told them

we fooled around."

He loosened his grip. The light from the full moon glinted off his gray eyes and I sucked in air. I hated how my body instantly reacted to his.

He told his friends what we did, yet I was turned on just being close to him. There was something wrong with me.

"I can't believe you did that."

He folded his arms, making him appear bigger, stronger, like he could lift me with little effort. My core hummed at the thought.

"So, you didn't tell Arabella? You've kept it a secret all week."

I rolled my lips over my teeth. "I may have."

"Then it's the same thing."

He had a point.

"Okay, I guess that was my bad. It's how he said it that—"

"There's one thing you should know about Caleb; he doesn't know when to keep his mouth shut. It really hasn't helped him with hanging on to girls."

That made sense.

"Okay. I have to get back. Arabella is going to be looking for me."

"No, she won't."

My eyebrows rose and a chill ran down my spine. "And why is that?"

"Take a look." He stepped aside and waved over to the far end of the parking lot where she was flirting with the footballs team.

"But we had plans tonight," I whispered.

And I really didn't want to be here anymore.

Something warm covered my shoulders. It was Knight's leather jacket.

"Thanks," I said, pulling it tight around me.

"Why don't I take you someplace to warm up?"

My clit had a brief spasm as he

whispered into my ear.

"A quickie in your car for half the school to see, no thank you."

"Not in a car." He slid his hand into mine and drew me closer to the woods. Why was I feeling like I was living a Grimm Fairytale?

We took a few steps in the woods. It was dark enough we wouldn't be seen, but the parking lot stayed in sight. Knight pushed me against a tree and then his body slammed into mine.

The leather protected my clothes from being torn up by the bark as he ground his hard cock into my thigh.

"I haven't stopped thinking about your pussy." He slid his fingers up my neck and into my hair, pulling my head back. "I bet it's so wet right now."

It was, but he didn't need to know that.

"Not really." I laughed, watching the annoyance flash in his eyes.

"You sure about that, Violet. I bet if I

slid my fingers down your jeans and touched your cotton panties, they'd be soaked."

My chest arched. I wanted what he was offering so badly but hearing the frustration in his voice made me even wetter.

"You think you're some kind of sex god, but you aren't."

His lips curled. "Look at you trying so hard to torture me." He bent his head, so his lips brushed my ear. "But we both know I'll be the one torturing you."

I pressed a finger to his chest and slid it down to the top of his jeans. "You're right. I really don't know what I'm doing."

He grabbed my finger and pushed my hand over the bulge in his jeans. I wanted to see what he looked like. What he felt like.

This was so messed up. I thought my first time would be with a guy I loved and who loved me back.

Not against a tree in the woods with a bully nicknamed the devil.

"You want this? You want me to tuck this deep inside you and make you come crying my name?"

I swallowed. My voice hoarse as I eked out a yes.

He unbuttoned my jeans and pull down the zipper. But right before he tugged them down, I stopped him.

"There's something you should know."

"Tell me now because you won't be able to say much once I fill you."

I nibbled on my thumbnail. "I'm a virgin."

He took a step back. "Really?"

I nodded.

His eyes darkened. "What is this? Did my uncle put you up to this?"

"What? You mean the man who almost raped me? Yes, I totally will do anything he tells me to do, including making his nephew take my virginity." I rolled my eyes.

He ran his fingers through his hair. "Violet, what my uncle did to you was terrible. And I know you wanted no part of it. But you have to understand, I know him. He gets people to do crazy things. People he's hurt and threatened will turn around and do his dirty work, no questions asked."

The mayor was worse than I thought.

"I'm sorry you have to live under his roof. I really am, but losing my virginity is my choice, not yours or your uncle's or anyone else's. And I choose you."

I gasped. Saying it out loud like that was a shock. I knew I wanted him and what we were doing would lead to sex, but to put it into words . . .. That made it real. Solid. There was no going back.

There was a slight tick at the corner of his mouth.

"Okay."

"And before you think I'm becoming

all mushy with you, I'm not. I'm attracted to you, that's it. If you want a girlfriend, go see Seraphina. She's dying to be your ankle bitch."

He chuckled. "I have to say, I almost lost it when I heard you say that to her."

We stood there for a moment, letting our laughter fade into the night.

"This is what you want?"

I was never one of those girls who dreamed of roses and sweetness for her first time. I imagined it hot and wild, and I knew that's what Knight could provide.

"Yes."

He didn't hesitate. His lips crashed onto mine. It was savage. Our lips couldn't get enough.

And just as fast as he started, Knight stopped. Our breaths were ragged as he leaned his forehead to mine. "This is your last warning. I don't fuck nice."

Fear and lust mingled in my throat "Yes, this is what I want."

EIGHTEEN

Violet

HE GRABBED MY NECK and pushed me back against the tree. This time I felt the hard ridges of the bark. His jacket had long since fallen from my shoulders.

There was pain with what he was doing

to my body, but instead of wishing to get away, I craved more.

"I was sweet to you in the locker room. But that was in case someone walked in. Here," he waved his hand at the trees, "no one will find us. No one will see what I will do to your body."

I swallowed and an unsettling shiver ran down my spine. My eye roamed wildly around the woods for signs of anyone close by. There was no one. I could see slivers of the parking lot, but it was too far for anyone to see us or hear me scream.

Was he like his uncle? Was I about to be raped?

He pulled up my thin sweater and pulled so hard on my bra cup that I heard a tear. My nipples were hard, I knew that. A mix of arousal and the cold air made them perfect to be played with.

But I suspected he didn't want to play.

Knight wanted to hurt me.

"Please," I whimpered.

His smile grew. "Oh no, is the little virgin changing her mind?"

The grip around my neck, never too tight that I couldn't breathe, loosened and slid down to twist my nipple. No cute tug and kneading, just bolts of pain ricocheting down my body.

My head went back as I cried out. After a moment it all turned to arousal and my cry turned into a whimper.

"You haven't answered me?"

I shook my head.

"Good, because I'm just getting started."

He did the same thing to my other nipple and I knew my panties were soaked. I squirmed but as I reached for him, he pushed my hands away.

"What I need you to do is take off your

clothes. I want to see everything I'm getting."

The ground wasn't soft with small sticks digging into my feet after I took off my shoes. My body shivered as I pulled off my jeans and panties. Once I threw my sweater and bra aside, I stood there as Knight studied me.

I should be embarrassed, but I wasn't. The way he watched me caused my body to burn. Eager for his touch, no matter how rough it may be.

"Fuck, you're gorgeous."

He unfastened his jeans and tugged them down, along with his briefs. They were dark in the wooded moonlight. Everything about Knight was dark.

His cock broke free and my eyes widened. He looked big and I wondered if I would fit him.

With a stroke of his cock, he smirked.

"Don't worry, Violet. You'll take me. And when I'm done, you'll beg for more. Now turn around and bend over."

What? Was that how he was going to do it? I felt disappointed. I wanted to kiss him and put my arms around him.

But I did as he said. I pressed my palms against the tree as I bent over.

"God, your ass is perfect. I can't wait to fuck it."

I whipped my head around. "I never said up the ass—"

A sudden crack of pain from Knight slap against my ass cheek shut me up. It hurt, but not much. It was after that I felt the shudder of intense desire flow over me. My clit twitched.

He scolded me with his touch. Branding me his, forever.

"Fuck," I groaned.

Then he shoved his fingers into my

core. Not like he had in the locker room, which was gentle compared to what he was doing now.

"God, you're so wet, you're dripping down my hand."

My mouth hung open as he worked me. He slid my wetness up and down, even circling my asshole. It should shock me. Recoil. But that dirty thought of him slipping inside my ass had me pushing myself into his hand.

"You're so dirty. Is that what my dirty girl wants? To be filled?"

I moaned and shook my ass.

"Fuck, Violet. When you told me you were a virgin, I really didn't want to do this with you. I like it rough and do some things virgins don't do. But, fuck, you're so dirty, and you haven't even been broken yet."

He slid two fingers into my core and

worked me, but I felt something pushing into my ass. A finger, maybe? I was so gone, groaning and grinding into him, I had no idea.

"I'm coming." I barely got it out as my climax slammed into me. It was more intense than the one before with Knight.

Wave after wave hit me even as his hands fell away from my body. I hardly heard him rip something open. Looking back, I saw he was rolling on a condom.

"This might hurt a little since you've never been fucked. But based on how much you love pain, I think you'll be okay."

He grabbed my ass and dug his fingers into my flesh. I felt the tip of his cock at my entrance. Then he rocked into me. It didn't take long until I felt a pinch. It was a twinge of pain, but he rocked his hips and soon it was gone.

"That's it. Warm and wet for me. Your pussy was begging to have me." He rocked in and out at a gentle pace, which surprised me.

The way Knight had been with my body, I thought he would pound into me. He felt incredible. Once the twinge of pain was gone, I was glad I chose him to be my first. To fuck me right.

I pushed against the tree to pick up the pace.

"Violet, easy. I know how you love my cock, but there're things I've got to do."

I felt his finger or thumb, something curve around the edge of my core where his cock was sliding in and out. He moved down and rubbed my clit.

"Yes," I cried out as I felt another orgasm build.

But right after I said that his finger left my clit, sliding up and down until it landed on my puckered hole again.

I glanced back. He was watching himself fuck me. He bit his lower lip. Knight was loving this as much as I was.

He glanced up. “I can’t reach your nipples. I need you to work them for me. And make it hurt, you dirty girl.”

I nodded and grabbed my left nipple, tugging and twisting. It didn’t compare to what Knight was doing to me, but it intensified everything.

Knight pressed something to my asshole again. I looked back and saw he was pushing his finger inside me. I could hardly breathe, it felt incredible. There was a slight burning when he first pushed inside, but once there, it went away.

The only way I could describe was that I felt was filled.

As he finger-fucked me in the ass, he picked up the pace with his cock.

"You're my new favorite toy, Violet. We're going to have so much fun together." His voice was hoarse, and I knew he would not last long.

Which was fine because I felt my orgasm coming. This time I couldn't say anything. Words evaporated from my lips as sheer ecstasy took over.

I cried out his name as I came.

"Oh, fuck, you're coming all over my cock. It's dripping down my leg. Fuck, you are so dirty."

Stars burst behind my eyelids as I rode out the intensity of the climax. His rhythm faltered and I heard him say my name as he pushed into me a few more times.

The aftershocks left me weak. My legs were giving way as he pulled out, but Knight held me in his arms.

It surprised me when he turned me around and kissed me. It was deep and filled with longing. Not rough like earlier, but soft.

He pulled his head back and gazed down at me. There was a hint of uncertainty that passed over his features before it disappeared into a cocky grin.

"How does it feel to be fucked right?"

Knight was basking in the glow of his mad sex skills. A little too sure of himself. But I didn't care. He deserved all the praise.

"Amazing."

"I was thinking since round one was over, why don't we head back home for round two."

I was about to say yes, but then I remembered why I was here to begin with. Arabella.

"I can't."

He stepped back, furrowing his brow. "You rather hang here at a stupid kegger at

Happy Pond then go home with me?"

"No, not at all. It's just that I came with Arabella and we had plans for after this."

"I think she'll understand."

I scratched an imaginary itch on the back of my neck.

"Look, Knight, she'd kill me if I told you, but we're going to see if we can find that hole in the basement floor. She's the one who told me about it."

He rubbed his chin and nodded. "Okay, but I'm coming with you."

"No, I don't think she'll like that—"

"I don't think you understand, Violet. I own you now. You wanted to be fucked by me. That means your pussy is mine. So, I'm coming."

NINETEEN

Violet

"I CAN'T BELIEVE YOU told him," Arabella whispered to me as she held the flashlight.

We were making our way through the boys' locker room in a darkened Green Hills Academy. I looked over at Knight, who was a few feet ahead of us.

To be honest, I couldn't believe it, either. But when he told me my pussy was his, I nearly groaned. That barbaric way of thinking should have repulsed me, but I got an intense thrill. I couldn't tell Arabella that.

"It irritated him that I wasn't sticking around."

She rolled her eyes. "If you hadn't given up your V-card to him, he wouldn't have found out about any of this."

"I told you we fooled around . . . I never said we had sex."

She snorted, pulling on the strap to the bag she had on her shoulder. "Oh please, it's written all over you euphoric-just-sexed expression."

I pursed my lips. "Fine. We had sex and it was amazing. But I figured he can pick locks. If that door is still locked, he can get us in. And besides, he's a big guy. If heavy furniture needs to be moved, he can do it."

She pondered what I said. "That is smart. But he might tell his buddies, and then word could get out to the entire school. Maybe if you keep fucking him, he'll grow a heart and not do anything to ruin us."

I'd keep fucking him, but not because I wanted him to stay quiet about what was in the basement. He was intensely good at doling out orgasms. I couldn't just walk away from that kind of talent.

"Shh." Knight put out his hand and stopped.

Arabella flashed her light around.

"Why did you shush us?" I asked.

"I thought I heard something. I guess it was nothing. Arabella, shine the light at the doorknob."

Knight got down on his knees and instantly, I flashed back to when he was down on his knees last time in the boys' locker room. Thankfully, it was dark, and no one could see the heat that was warming my face.

Knight didn't use his necklace this time. He pulled out a few long picks and maneuvered them around the keyhole. The door clicked and he pulled it open.

Once inside, Knight flipped a switch lighting the way and we turned off the flashlights.

When we got down the stairs to the basement, Arabella said, "Oh my god, this place looks so spooky."

She had a huge grin on her face. I guess the girl liked scary stuff.

"Where do you think the hole would be?" I asked.

Arabella reached into her bag and lifted out some pieces of paper. "Now, according to the surveyor's map I got a hold of—"

I held up my hands. "Hold up. Surveyor's map? When did that happen?"

"Last year. I was doing a history paper on the building, totally sucking up to Mr.

Krantz for an A. He loves all things Green Hills. So, I thought, why not do a paper on the place? What I found was interesting. That's why I think the shaft is still here."

She walked over to an old school desk and laid out the sheets of paper.

"See, this here is the map from 1900. But this one is from 2000. There're some changes, but you see this line that leads to the river? That's the shaft." She traced the dotted line with her finger.

Knight came and stood next to me. His hand slid onto my lower back. I glanced over to Arabella, but she was too busy studying to map to notice.

A shiver ran down to my core, causing me to shift from his touch.

"It's still there," Knight whispered close to my ear.

"Am I the only one feeling like we're in a Scooby Doo episode?" I let out a stilted laugh and stepped away from Knight.

"We better watch out for old Mr.

Oakley, the groundskeeper, then." Arabella chuckled.

"If the two of you are done joking, let's get to work." Knight's eyes bore into me as he held up a map. "According to this, it should be right over here."

He walked over to where there were old desks and chairs piled on top of each other. My lower back still hummed from where he touched me. I shook my head and did my best to focus on the work and not the devil.

We all got to work moving the old furniture.

Knight took away the last desk and we saw a rug on the floor.

"Why would there be a rug on a cement floor . . .?" I asked.

Knight had a mischievous grin. "Why don't we roll it up and find out?"

What we found under it surprised us.

"Just an old piece of plywood? That's what separating us from the hole?"

Arabella asked.

"That seems dangerous. Maybe that's why no one was allowed down here."

Knight ignored the two of us and pushed the large board out of the way.

"That's a handle," I said with a gasp.

It was old, rusty, and round. It lay on the floor and was attached to a hinge.

Knight pointed down. "The more important observation is that's a door."

The hinge was bolted to a very heavy-looking door, and it seemed old. Based on the rust pattern, it was made of wood and iron.

"I don't think we can lift it," Arabella added.

To come all this way and not even be able to open the door. To say it frustrated me was an understatement.

"Let's at least try." Knight reached down and pulled. He almost fell back as the door popped right open.

"That was much easier than I thought

it would be."

A cool blast of damp air wafted up the dark hole.

I bent over the hole and squinted. "It's pitch-black down there. How are we going to tell if it leads to the stream?"

"Maybe if you just jump down and check." Knight's hands went to my shoulders and gave a slight push, but never let go.

I yelled and scurried back. His head went back as he roared with laughter.

I folded my arms over my chest and scowled at him. "That wasn't funny. I could have slipped and fell in."

His chuckles faded. "No, you wouldn't. I had you the entire time."

"Okay, goofballs, let's keep at this. We can use our flashlights." Arabella turned hers on and pointed it into the dark hole.

We all did. If I thought the old basement was creepy, it didn't compare to the shoot. It reminded me of a water slide that was old and covered in moss.

I covered my nose because the smell that was coming from it was vile. The longer we stood there, the stronger it grew.

"There must be some dead animals down there." Arabella frowned.

"Does anyone have anything small we can throw down there to hear how far it goes?" I dug into my pockets and found nothing.

Arabella grabbed her bag from the floor and dug inside. "Hey, I have some change. Here's a penny."

She handed it to me, and I held it over the hole before I let go. There were some clinks that sounded farther and farther away until there was nothing.

"If it still went all the way to the stream, it should have gone longer. Something is blocking it," Knight said.

"I bet it's just sealed up. Maybe stuff got stuck down there over time. Who's ready to head out? Violet, you want to come over? I could order pizza." Arabella shrugged her bag onto her shoulder.

"You're leaving?" Knight asked.

"Yeah, what else is there to do? I only wanted to find it. It's not like I had big plans to stuff bodies down there," Arabella said with a laugh.

I chuckled, but it faded the moment I realized Knight wasn't laughing.

"Don't tell me you plan to bury bodies down here?" I asked and swallowed, uncertain as to how he would answer.

"None that you know of." His lips curled.

"Okay. Creepy. Totally going to leave now. Violet, you coming with?"

"We're just going to keep the enormous gaping hole here? What if a janitor comes down in the morning or your father?" I waved at Arabella.

"I'll clean up. You two leave. I wanted to check on a few things before I left."

Arabella placed her arm around me, pulling me toward the stairs.

She leaned over and whispered, “He probably brought a tape measure. Wants to see if he can fit a body down there. I admit, he’s hot, and I don’t blame you for letting Knight snatch that V-card with gusto. But—”

“But what?”

We made it to the top of the stairs when she stopped me and placed her hands on my shoulders. “He has never been the same since his parents died. Sure, he was the typical spoiled rich kid before, but now . . .. Let’s just say if a body showed up here, he’d be the first person on my suspect list.”

I nibbled at my lip because a part of me thought Arabella was right about Knight.

TWENTY

Violet

"**Oh my god, can** you believe they have an on-site spa facility with massages available any time of the day or night?" Arabella said as we made our way back to the bus.

"I know and the campus is beautiful." I

spun around, soaking in the gorgeous mountains that framed the campus.

Today was the senior field trip and we were enjoying the day at Winter River University. As I found out from our college guide, Green Hills Academy was the only school in the country allowed to tour the campus.

Arabella and I strolled up to the bus. The door was open, but our driver wasn't around. I checked my cell phone. "We're a little early."

"Really? Because there's an ice cream cone vendor just across the quad." Arabella pouted.

"Honestly, I'm full from the sushi bar in the dining hall. You go get your ice cream, I'll wait on the bus."

She clapped her hands, "Yay. I promise I won't be long."

Arabella hitched up her backpack and dashed off. I waited out in front of the bus but there was a chill from the cool early autumn breeze that had me eying the warm seats inside. It was much cooler up here in the mountains then back at Green Hills.

I glanced around to see if anyone else was coming back.

No one. I was both relieved and disappointed. All the seniors, except for Knight, went on the field trip. I guess if your family founded the university, you didn't need a tour.

But he wasn't the reason I was relieved, it was Seraphina. She had been extra salty to me today. The entire bus ride was her and her friends, making comments about how I was too poor to even consider going to Winter River. That it was sad how I was tormenting myself by attending the field trip.

I did my best to ignore her and the rest of kids on the bus as they laughed at whatever Seraphina said about me. But by the end of the bus ride, she was getting under my skin.

The beautiful campus and the wonderful people I met at Winter River helped me forget about Seraphina once we toured the campus.

I sighed as I stepped up the steps into the lavish, chartered bus. Another Seraphina reminder—her family donated the bus to the school just for the seniors.

The seats were wide and plush. Each had its own little table. And there was a bathroom in the back that didn't smell like a used diaper.

The driver parked the bus on an angle as the parking lot was on a slope since the campus took up the side of a mountain. I held onto the seats as I made my way to mine in the empty bus.

When we toured the marketing department, I got into a discussion with a professor. I impressed her with how I ran the social media accounts in my old school. When I went to South Green High, all they had was a Socialbook account where they posted pictures of the faculty smiling at their desks.

When I joined the media club at South Green, I suggested we take over the school's social media sites. I got the school on HitLoc, and after working with the cheerleaders, we were trending doing routines to old songs.

The marketing professor gave me her email and told me to reach out in a few days. I was hoping she might put in a kind word for me so I'd get the chance to apply.

The sound of giggling caught my attention and as I looked up, my heart fell. It was Seraphina and her bitch squad.

"I knew it smelled like a dead rat in here," she sneered at me.

Not even Seraphina was going to bring me down on the ride home. I was one step closer to getting into my dream school.

"You're so original, Seraphina. You must have the biggest brain in the world to come up with that. Rats. So clever." I smirked.

They didn't go to their seats, just hung by the door. One of her friends kept looking back outside, like they were waiting for someone.

"You know Knight came to visit me last night. That's probably why he isn't here today. So tired. We were up all night," she said with a yawn.

"Right." I rolled my eyes.

I had noticed Knight wasn't there when I went to bed last night. Since we fucked at the party on Saturday, almost a week ago, he came into my room every night this week, except for last night.

Seraphina frowned. "I'm sorry. He told me not to tell you."

Glancing out the window, I searched for Arabella but I couldn't find her.

"He wanted his USB drive back."

"What are you even talking about, Seraphina?"

Like Knight having a USB drive meant anything to me. Most people had one.

One of her friends, the one I called brunette bitch, tugged on Seraphina's sleeve. "Come on, Seraphina, we have to go."

"Alright, Dani. I know. I just need to tell Violet how Knight was the one with the footage of her naked in the pool house."

I blinked as a pounding erupted in my ears.

"That's not true."

My mind raced back to the day when the mayor and his creepy buddies tried to rape me. When I saw Knight coming out of the pool house that evening with something in his hand.

Had he planted a camera in my bedroom? It made sense because why else would he sneak into the pool house after I left. Knight must have gone back in to remove the camera.

"So, he put the footage in the school

film?" I asked more to myself than to Seraphina, but she heard me.

"No, that bit of mastery was me. Well, the film student I hired. It's amazing what a college student would do for fifty bucks."

I stood and marched toward the bus door. There was no Arabella around to hold me back from punching Seraphina in the face.

"You fucking bitch!" I screamed as I stood at the top of the three steps that led to the ground.

She stepped back, along with her squad, and lifted her key ring. Seraphina pressed her key fob and the doors to the bus closed. I ran down the steps and pushed.

She had locked the doors. I banged on them and yelled at the top of my lungs, "Let me out!"

She shook her head and laughed. Seraphina waved at me and mouthed, "Bye, bitch," before her and her friends strolled away.

Taking a few breaths, I gave up on the door and went back up the steps. Once I made it to my seat, I was too angry to enjoy the leaves on the trees changing colors or the red brick buildings.

Knight was lying to me. For a guy who wanted me to stay, he was doing his best to mess with my head. I hated that when I saw him warmth bloomed between my thighs.

I hated him. Despised his very being. But when he touched me, all I wanted to do was rip his clothes off.

I coughed out a hard laugh. Of course, he was the one who filmed me naked in my bedroom. He was all too eager to film me almost being raped. Knight played it off like he rescued me. That was bullshit.

Maybe the reason he wanted me to stay wasn't to protect me at all. It was to film me getting raped.

He used his sister as an excuse. To pull

on my heartstrings. But it wasn't for that at all.

He wanted me in the house because the mayor, and maybe even him too, could just walk right into my bedroom and have their way with me. There was nowhere I could hide. Not even that attic.

Hot tears trickled down my cheeks. I wanted to roll up into a ball and disappear. Once the trip was over, I was taking Arabella up on her offer. I would not spend another night in the King home.

Glancing out the window, I saw Arabella holding a large waffle cone in her hand, licking the blue ice cream piled on top. She saw me and waved. From that distance, she couldn't tell I was crying. That Seraphina had won. That the queen bitch had broken me.

I lifted my shaking hand to wave back, but then I noticed the scene outside move. Arabella stopped and lowered her cone.

It wasn't the outside moving, it was me.

The bus was rolling down the hill. Arabella dropped her cone and ran toward the bus. But what could she do?

I pushed out of my seat and pulled myself toward the front. It wasn't easy. With the bus rolling, the incline increased, making it hard to move toward the front of the bus.

It took some strength, but I got down the steps and pushed on the door. It wouldn't budge. No matter how much I kicked or shoved, the doors remained closed.

My head whipped around as I frantically searched for an emergency release button.

I found nothing.

There was a pain in my chest as I realized I was trapped. Despite not finding any release button, I pushed and pulled anything I found, just in case.

Within seconds, I pulled myself into the driver's seat. The bus bumped and I heard horns blaring as the bus rolled out of the parking lot and into traffic.

I did my best to steer as I was going backward in a large bus. It helped, and the wheels turned easily. I just had to maneuver the thing to a spot that was flat and away from other cars.

My feet pressed the pedals on the floor, hoping to discover the brake pedal. All the pedals went straight to the floor—they had no pressure.

I grit my teeth as I cursed to myself. No matter what I pressed or pulled, nothing worked.

As I keep watch in the rear-view mirror, I notice a flat area just around the curve of the road. Sucking in a breath, I steadied myself for the only option I had to stop the bus.

It would require me to cut through to the other side of the road, but what choice did I have left?

I was sweating so much I thought I

would pass out. Blinking, I noticed a small opening in the cars and jerked the wheel. There was one catch with this option—at the end of the flat bit of road was a guardrail with nothing on the other side of it. Just a drop off the mountain.

The bus bounced as it ran over the curb and onto the flat surface. I hoped the curb slowed the thing down. There was nothing I could do but buckle myself in and wait for my fate.

I scrambled to grab the seat belt and after a few frantic attempts, I got the buckle secure. If the bus went over, at least I wouldn't see it. I closed my eyes and held onto the seat belt as if that would help.

The bus slowed, but what slowed it was the guardrail. I heard metal scraping and I chanted the word *please* repeatedly. There was a bump and the bus tilted.

But it finally stopped.

I let out the longest breath of my life. Turning my head, I saw cars and people.

They had stopped to come help. A police car showed up, too.

I was about to reach for my belt buckle when the bus tilted even more. The bus made a loud groan and a horrific scrapping sound.

I glanced back right at the moment that the bus slipped over the ledge. It raced down the side of the mountain. My body bounced and the only thing I could make out were trees, lots of them. The bus was racing toward them.

There was a thump right before everything went black.

TWENTY-ONE

Violet

"VIOLET, HONEY, THANK GOD you're okay," Aunt Dahlia said as she came to my side.

I blinked. It was white. An annoying beeping sound kept going off.

"Shut that off," I mumbled trying to lift

my arm, but a shooting pain stopped me.

"Violet, just rest. Do you remember what happened?"

"Huh?"

I tried to turn my head, but something prevented me from moving. A memory flashed in my head.

The bus.

"Do you remember the crash?"

I stared at my aunt, confused at what she was talking about. My brain felt foggy like when I was sixteen and had to get my wisdom teeth removed. The dentist gave me a drug that made it hard to form any thoughts. "I-I don't remember."

My mouth was dry. I kept licking my lips.

"Perfect timing. I see she's awake," a woman said as she walked into the room.

She had red, wavy hair and smiled.

"I'm Doctor Phillips. Do you know why you're here, Violet?"

"No." My eyes roamed the room. "I'm

thirsty."

"I'll have the nurse give you some water."

Both Aunt Dahlia and I listened as the doctor told me I had clavicle fracture and whiplash. That's why it hurt when I tried to lift my arm.

"How long will she have to wear the brace on her neck?" my aunt asked.

"Only for a few more days. But the arm brace will be a few weeks. Then I'll prescribe physical therapy."

My aunt nodded and placed her hand on mine.

"Why don't I remember?"

I wanted to remember what had happened, but all I knew was not being able to get off that bus. *But why?*

The doctor sighed. "I think part of the memory loss is because of the pain medication you're on. You've been in and out of sleep for the last twelve hours."

What? It's been twelve hours. The last

thing I could remember outside of the bus was being at Winter River University. But I had no memory of why I was there.

"And the other part?" my aunt asked.

"The accident. Violet, you hit your head pretty hard. That's why you're still here. We're going to keep you for the next twelve hours. After your aunt approved the CT scan, we found you had a concussion."

I wanted to leave and figure out what had happened but keeping my eyes open was exhausting. I must have fallen back asleep because when I opened my eyes again, my aunt was gone and Arabella was sitting in the chair next to my bed.

"Oh my god, you're awake."

"Yes." I blinked. "Water."

My mouth felt like a desert on a sunny July day.

"Right. Your aunt told me you had asked for water before." She reached over to a table beside my bed that I hadn't realized was there and held up the Styrofoam cup with a straw.

It was embarrassing having to rely on someone to get me water. But once the refreshing liquid hit my tongue, I realized it was worth all the shame.

A short time later, she pulled the cup away.

"Sorry, the nurse said not to have too much. You might get sick. And while I don't mind giving you water, even feeding you, I will not clean up your puke. Sorry, there's a line a girl won't cross." She winked.

I tried to smile, but it was hard. My face felt stiff and swollen. Ugh, I probably looked like a drunken clown from the accident.

"What happened?" I asked. My voice was louder this time, but groggy.

"You were in the bus when it rolled away. We were all confused why you didn't jump out. Not to mention how the bus started rolling downhill to begin with. Seraphina told us her dad fired the driver."

A memory came back.

"Seraphina . . ." I mumbled.

Arabella nodded. "Yes, she tore into the driver. Man, you should have seen it. She told him she endangered the life of a fellow student and could have had us all killed. As if she cared about you. I think she was just saying all that to not look like the harpy that got the bus that brought you to the hospital."

I tried shaking my head but remembered I had the brace on. "No, Seraphina locked me in the bus."

I gulped breaths. It wasn't easy talking.

"What? She said her and her friends were hanging by the fountain when they saw the bus roll away. That lying bitch." Arabella pushed her hands on her hips.

"You have a visitor." The nurse showed up and just behind her was Knight.

My stomach twisted and a sense of unease washed over me. Seraphina told me something about Knight, but I couldn't remember what it was.

"Hi." He waved before running his fingers through his hair. "Looks like I missed all the fun."

"Yeah, it was crazy. And Violet just told me that Seraphina locked her on the bus."

His nose flared. "Why?"

Arabella shrugged. "Because she's a bitch."

Knight turned his steely gray gaze on me. I blinked, frustrated that I couldn't remember what Seraphina had said to me. Why had she locked me on the bus?

"I don't know."

Knight let out a breath. Maybe it was the pain meds, but he seemed relieved.

"Her aunt said she had trouble remembering things about the accident."

"Is she still here?" My mouth was getting dry again and I eyed the cup of water.

"She went home to change and shower. She came straight here from Wichita and stayed all night with you. I told her to get some rest and that I'd call her when it was time to pick you up." Arabella smiled.

"But you live with me," Knight said, his voice laced with irritation.

"Uh, it's her aunt."

Knight took a step forward, slipping his hand over mine. "But she lives with me. She's been living with me for weeks. I can take care of her."

Take care of her. My heart pounded in my chest. Memories of when my mom died and his uncle came racing back.

"No. I want to be with my aunt," I said with a whimper.

"But, Violet, your clothes, all your school stuff, everything is there in your room." He leaned closer, refusing to take his eyes off me.

"But I want to be with my aunt right

now. I miss her."

Knight turned to Arabella. "Can you give a few minutes?"

Arabella looked at me. "Can I, Violet?"

What could he do to me in a hospital? I grumbled out a yes and Arabella turned to leave. But as she got to the doorway, she said, "I'll be right in the hallway."

She left and Knight turned back to me.

"What if my uncle finds out you're staying with your aunt? He might think you're going to tell."

I knew that, but I didn't care.

"I've just been in a bus accident. I can't even remember how it happened or why I was at Winter River University to begin with. I want comfort. That's not what I feel when I'm in your home."

I gasped for breath after my brief speech.

He groaned. "But I can protect you. I can't protect your aunt or you in your aunt's house."

I rolled my eyes. "Okay, Superman."

"I'm serious, Violet. If you stay with your aunt, it's risky."

Taking a deep breath, I said, "It's a risk I'm willing to take."

He paced the room. "I got money and can have anything you need brought to the house. I could hire an at-home nurse to take care of you."

Why did he care so much? I wanted to ask him, but it was difficult to talk. And I was growing tired.

"Can we discuss this another time? I need rest."

He marched up to my bed and pointed into my face. "The only reason I'm letting this happen is because you were almost killed. The moment you feel better is the moment you come back to the house."

He turned and strolled out the door, punching the wall as he left.

"What the hell?" Arabella said with a sneer. "What crawled up his ass and died?

Oh, right . . . it's his soul."

"I told him I was staying with my aunt."

"And he got that mad? What a controlling psycho. Don't worry, Violet, I'll make sure he stays away from you."

I mumbled something, but my eyelids grew heavy. Thoughts of what Seraphina had said to me on the bus before she locked me inside danced around my head.

Knight was the one with the footage.

TWENTY-TWO

Knight

"THERE'S A YOUNG WOMAN at the front entrance to see you, Mr. King," Hugh, my new butler, mentioned as he came into the kitchen.

I nodded to Hugh, who turned and left.

"You think that's Violet? She's coming

back, right?" Ava frowned and crossed her fingers on both hands.

"Yes, she's coming back, just like I promised. But I don't know if that's her."

Violet needed some time to heal. Then she'd realize how much safer she was here. Especially when I explained that she never had to worry about my uncle stepping foot in this home ever again.

I slid off the bar stool and patted Ava's back. "You stay here. If it's Violet, I'll send Hugh for you."

It had been a week since the bus crash. Violet wasn't speaking to me. She left the hospital five days ago. When I saw her in that hospital bed, I wanted to punch someone.

That accident shouldn't have happened.

I told Violet I'd protect her and the one day I wasn't around she was almost killed.

That bus incident was a mess. It was made to look like an accident, but to someone like me, it looked very much on purpose.

I meandered to the front entrance. Bile rose in my throat as my eyes landed on the person waiting for me.

"Seraphina. What are you doing here?"

She gave me her usual sly grin. She thought she looked cute, but I thought she looked pathetic.

"Knight, I came to bring you a housewarming gift." She held out a small box in her palm.

It looked like a ring box wrapped in blue paper with a small white bow on top.

"I don't need a gift."

She took a step closer and slid her hand down my arm. I jerked away.

"Baby, I know you don't need anything." She waved her arms around the room. "Not since all this is now yours. You're welcome by the way."

I flattened my lips. "It was a deal. That's it. I already promised I would follow through when the time comes."

I hated that I owed Seraphina and if she kept holding it over my head, I might have to forget about the agreement.

"You will. And in the meantime, I thought we could celebrate with some sparkling wine in your room." She tried to reach for me again, but I backed away.

"Seraphina, thanks for helping with transferring the deed of the house into my name. Legally, this house became mine once I turned eighteen according to my parents' will, but I knew my uncle would make it difficult and try to claim that I had no right. I'm happy your father could help me with the paperwork."

"Now, was that so hard?" she

murmured in her annoying baby voice.

My nose flared and I glanced back toward the hallway that led to the kitchen. Ava wasn't lurking about, thankfully. But that didn't mean she wouldn't be soon. She had a habit of not listening to me and letting her curiosity take over.

I smiled as I realized how much Ava was like me.

"Yes, it was hard."

Seraphina rolled her eyes. "Whatever. Just open your gift."

"Will you leave after?"

She pushed her hands on her hips, causing her fake tits to jet out. "I know your trashy new girlfriend isn't here. We can fool around. I can suck you off just how you like it." She slid her finger down her throat.

My stomach twisted. "We broke up months ago. Why can't you accept that?"

Seraphina stomped her foot and growled, "Really, Knight? You chose that slutty piece of garbage over me? You know she's just using you, right?"

"You know nothing, Seraphina."

She folded her arms over her chest and let out a forced laugh. "My mom know everything that goes on in this town. Did you know that she tried to have sex with the mayor and his friends all at the same time? She's such a slut. Probably thought they could be her sugar daddies."

"Shut the fuck up. You don't understand what you're talking about."

Her lips curled. "I know exactly what I'm talking about. And so do you. I mean, you're the one who filmed it."

That fucking bitch.

I grabbed her by the arm and pulled her into the library, shutting the door, and slamming her against it.

She pushed her tits into me and moaned, “Yes, Knight. Please—”

“You’re sick, you know that?” I slid my fingers into her hair, pulling her head back. But I wasn’t delicate about it.

Her smile faded to a scowl. “Fuck, you’re hurting me.”

“That’s right, I am. So, you thought you could mess with me? Take my phone and go through my things. I wonder what would happen if I went through yours, hmm. What would I find?”

Her eyes widened and there was unadulterated fear staring back at me. “No. Knight. You wouldn’t.”

I slid my finger down from her ear until my hand was gripping her throat. I felt her swallow, and if it was earlier this year, I’d be hard. But nothing about Seraphina turned me on anymore.

Seraphina made me happy in another

life—a life when I hated the world and all the people in it.

For the past two years I had a crash course in the sick and twisted lives of the adults around me. She eased the pain from that knowledge.

But I realized she knew about all the crazy shit that went on in this town, and she didn't care.

As I stared at one offspring of those fucked-up adults, I shuddered at what I avoided becoming.

"I know what you like, Seraphina. We dated for a year, and I know all your dark and messed-up secrets. Just try to threaten me again and see what happens."

She pushed me back and with a shaky hand, wiped the tear from her cheek.

"Fuck you, Knight. You're no saint. You're just as twisted as me."

"I'm sure that's why everyone calls me

the devil." I grinned.

"So that's it." Seraphina threw her hands up. "I get one night after giving you this place."

I nodded. "That was the deal you agreed to."

She turned her back to me and after a few seconds, she screamed. It wasn't ear piercing like she did when she was pretending to get hurt so she could get someone in trouble. Her howl was deep and angry.

She opened the library door and marched out. Right before she reached for the front door to leave, she turned back. "If you think this is over, you're crazy. Just know that I haven't even started."

Seraphina left and slammed the front door behind her. I chuckled and wondered what sad little ideas that girl thought she could come up with to scare me.

Unlike her, I didn't care what anyone thought of me. Her love of spreading false rumors would have no effect on me. And I doubt she could get anyone to call me names at school.

"A present! Yay. I love presents."

Ava walked over with Seraphina's gift in her hand. I was about to tell her not to open it, but I should have known better. She liked to rip wrapping paper away first and ask questions later.

The paper was already shredded and on the floor by the time I turned to face Ava. She lifted the black velvet ring box and frowned.

"Eww."

I reached for the box. When I saw what it was, my mouth fell open.

"It's a tooth. Is it a shark's tooth? My friend Jacob has a necklace with a shark's tooth, but his looks pointy." Ava continued to ramble as I stared at the thin gold chain with a human tooth dangling from it.

When I lifted it up the padding popped out and behind it was a folded-up piece of paper. I opened the letter and read:

Not only did you get the house you wanted, but you got your wish, too. Violet is gone.

I swallowed. That was what I had wished for.

TWENTY-THREE

Violet

"HE'S OUTSIDE AGAIN," AUNT Dahlia said.

"I told you, I don't want to see him. Tell Knight to leave or I'm calling the police."

I groaned as I pulled myself up from the couch. I missed a week of school, but the principal and my teachers understood. Knight had been stopping by every evening with takeout and my textbooks.

I hadn't asked him to come by and since it's Saturday, there was no reason to drop off schoolwork.

"Knight seems sweet. Isn't he the boy who found you at the pond?"

I nodded, wincing. My shoulder and neck still hurt, but it was nothing a little over-the-counter medicine wouldn't help. I wore a sling on my arm but hadn't worn the neck brace in five days.

When I looked in the mirror after the accident, my appearance horrified me. And even more in shock that Arabella had said nothing to me. She could have at least brought a hairbrush to the hospital. I still had bits of leaves in my hair when I left.

I looked a lot better since then. The swelling and most of the bruising had faded. I just had some yellowing around my eye.

"Unfortunately."

Dahlia sighed. "I told you you'd find a boy when you got to Green Hills. And he's very good-looking." Her brows rose and fell.

I snorted. "Please stop, you're embarrassing yourself."

She gave me the Adler smile. "Everything I predicted came true. You found a friend. Arabella has come over to visit every day. So, there's no denying that you two are friends."

I bit my lip. "She's cool. The only decent person in that school."

"It would never be easy, you knew that."

I gave a hard laugh. "The understatement of the millennium."

"Yes, the bus accident was scary. But

you lived. And, if this letter is any sign, you're one step closer to your dream." She held up an envelope with the address label of Winter River University.

I yelped and reached over, grabbing it from her hand.

In my excitement, I forgot it was difficult for me to open the letter. "Uh . . . can you help me."

I could use my finger, but it was painful. It was just easier to get someone else to open mail.

"Anything for my favorite niece." Dahlia ripped it open and pulled out the letter, handing it over.

I nibbled on my lip. What if Winter River found out I missed a week of school? They were particular about attendance.

Shit. That hadn't occurred to me this past week when I was lying in bed in pain and feeling sorry for myself. I should have sucked it up and went to school.

My hand shook as I unfolded the letter.

It was so shaky I couldn't read it.

"I can't." I handed it over to my aunt.

"I'll do it." She cleared her throat. "Dear Ms. Violet Adler. We are excited to inform you we have selected you as a small group of people invited to apply, with scholarship, to Winter River University. We have been a university since—"

I cut my aunt off as I screamed. I would have jumped up and down, but it hurt my shoulder. Tears of joy were meandering down my cheeks.

"Does that mean you got in?"

I shook my head with a wince. "No, they invite you to apply first. And this is the invitation. They only have a select group of people they allow to apply and from that, they make their decision. But I got my foot in the door."

I wiped at my tears as my aunt gave me a hug. Finally getting some good news after so many horrible weeks was wonderful.

Maybe something good would come out of me going to Green Hills.

There was pounding coming from the front door that broke our joyful celebration.

My aunt went to check it out.

"What's going on. Is she hurt?" I heard Knight yell.

I groaned. He would not stop. No matter how much I ignored him, he wouldn't leave me alone. It was time to shut him down.

When I got to the front door, he stood there glaring at my aunt.

"Stop trying to scare her, it won't work," I said and placed my hand on her shoulder.

"Why don't I give you two some time to talk." She nodded and stepped back, heading into the kitchen.

"I'd let you in, but we have a strict no assholes policy." I leaned against the door.

Knight stood there, his body practically vibrating from irritation. "Why haven't you responded to me? I've texted you and have come here every day. What did I do?"

I narrowed my eyes. "You know exactly what you did."

Knight threw his hands up, letting out an exasperated sigh.

"No, I really don't. Last I checked, I was keeping you safe in my home. And it's my home now. Once I turned eighteen, it became mine. I finally signed the papers. My uncle can't get into the house. I will have him arrested if he tries."

My head jerked back. “Really? You own that enormous mansion?”

“Yes, it was my parents. But once my uncle took over as our caregiver, he made it his. Even tried to circumnavigate my parents’ will to claim he should be on the deed. But my mom, being a Saget, had the best lawyers. Any deed or contract or will that had her name on it was airtight. He couldn’t do anything. I suspect that’s why he’s been on vacation for so long. He knew he didn’t have a house to come home to.”

I rubbed my forehead. “That’s crazy. So, I don’t have to worry about your uncle coming after me anymore?”

He sighed, leaning against the door frame. “I never said that. Here’s the thing, Violet. My uncle is a powerful guy. He still has money of his own. But he won’t be able to get into my house. I brought in an entirely new staff, had all the locks changed, and put in new security. Inside my home, you're safe. Outside . . . I don't know."

I glanced back toward the kitchen. My aunt wasn't there. I hope she hadn't heard Knight.

"But the footage of me," I lowered my voice, "getting undressed in the pool house. The one that was shown at the rally a couple of weeks ago. That was from you."

"No, that was from my uncle." He rubbed his face. "He installed those cameras in the pool house. After what he did to you, I went into the pool house later that night and removed the cameras. I went into his office after you fell asleep that evening and got onto his computer. That's when I saw the video link up to the pool house. I took them away and removed the footage from my uncle's computer."

"Then why did Seraphina say you gave it to her?"

"Because she's a psycho bitch who hates you. What she failed to mention was that she got the footage from my locker. I kept that stuff in my gym locker because those are the only lockers in the school that don't get random searches. And my uncle would never get access to it. If I kept it in the house, he might find it."

That made sense. But there was something I was still confused about.

"When you caught me in the locker room, I heard Seraphina. But that was after the rally."

He smirked. "She was putting back the things she stole. Thought I wouldn't notice them missing, but I did. I punished her. There was a reason I wasn't on the field trip. I was there at Winter River, but not to see the sights. She'll discover soon enough that it's not wise to mess with me." His features darkened.

Everything made sense now. It wasn't Knight fucking with me, but Seraphina.

He reached out and slid his finger down my cheek. My skin broke out in goose pimples down my back. He leaned in and I inhaled his spicy cologne. "I miss you."

My nipples hardened. He was warm and all I wanted to do was reach for him.

"Why me?" I asked, still unsure.

"You're different."

I kicked the door frame. "You mean I'm not a spoiled brat."

He slipped his fingers under my chin, lifting my head until I gazed into his glittering gray eyes.

"That's not what I meant. You're real. You don't care what these rich bastards think of you. I see it in your eyes. The world hurt you and instead of letting it crush you, you fought back." He sighed, staring at my lips. "I know what that's like."

Fuck. My heart cracked a little.

"Why did you stay the night at Seraphina's before the bus accident. She told me you came to her. If you hated her, why stay the night?" I raised a brow at him.

"Her father. He helped me arrange the house to be in my name. Nothing between us happened no matter how much she wanted to paint it that way. After, I went and hung out with my friends. That's all. You still want to fight about things that aren't true?"

My shoulders sagged.

"I'm tired of fighting," I whispered.

"Me, too." He leaned forward and kissed me.

It was a whisper. A kiss that spoke

about heartache and loss. It was like being seen for the very first time.

He slipped his hand around my waist and pulled me close.

"Let me in, Violet. I promise, I won't let the mayor or anyone else hurt you."

I nodded and let him in the door. I believed him. Only it wasn't the mayor I was worried about at that moment. It was my heart and what Knight would do to it.

TWENTY-FOUR

Violet

"**DID YOU HEAR WHAT** happened? Why school was closed on Monday?" Arabella asked as she pulled up to Knight's house.

My aunt and I moved into his home right after I talked to him on Saturday. He was honest with Aunt Dahlia—or as honest as he could be. I didn't want her to know about what the mayor and his buddies did to me. He kept that part secret.

It mortified her that she let me live with him. I told her that's why I was worried about her when I hadn't heard from her those days around my birthday.

She explained she got a terrible case of food poisoning and was in the hospital. She never told me because she didn't want me to worry.

With the mayor as my enemy, that's all I ever did was worry.

"No, what happened?"

I slid into her car and she took off. Arabella glanced around as she turned into traffic.

"I overheard my father on the phone."

I snorted. "You mean you eavesdropped on your father."

She waved her hand at me.

"Overheard, eavesdropped, same difference. Anyway, they found a body in the basement. In that hole."

"Holy shit," I breathed.

My mind raced, wondering if we locked back up. Would the police question us since we found it a few weeks ago?

"Apparently, the body's been there for a while. That's how the janitor found it. The smell." Arabella scrunched up her face.

"It smelled when we were down there . . .. Do you think the body was already there?"

"It might have been. I'm going to spend lunch helping my father." She winked. "Maybe I can find more information."

"Good idea."

We spent the rest of the car ride coming up with various theories on the body. Arabella thought it might be the mayor as he hasn't been seen since the day he tried to rape me.

I didn't think it would be him. Knight would have figured something out. That's when she suggested Knight might have killed him.

"He used to have lots of anger issues, Violet. They put him in an institution for a few months . . . about six months after his parents died. Like I said before, he's not the same."

I knew he was angry, but I had no idea it ever got that bad for him.

"No, it couldn't have been him. He got the house and his sister's safe. There's no way he would kill the mayor. Not because he tried to rape me."

Arabella sighed. "Okay, I'm going to tell you something, but you can't tell Knight. Like, at all."

I nodded. “Okay.”

“I’m so fucking serious, Violet.” She came to a stop in the line of cars for the valet at school.

We noticed a few police cars parked in the parking lot. We would probably see more of them over the next few days as they swept the basement.

“Everyone here thinks Knight went to the institution because he tried to off himself. He didn’t. They informed my father that Knight tried to kill his uncle. He tried to poison his food.”

I sucked in a breath. “Holy shit. What happened? The mayor didn’t die.”

“He went to the hospital. At first, he thought it was food poisoning. Like he ate bad chicken or something. But when they took a blood sample, they found something in his blood. The mayor thought one of his staff tried to poison him, so he had the house searched and found rat poison in Knight's room. After that, he was shipped off for several months. When he came back, he was . . . different."

After Knight and I talked this past weekend, he was so kind and offered for my aunt to move in. How could a guy like that try to kill someone?

"He said nothing to me," I murmured.

She pulled up to the front and the valet attendants opened the door.

"Why would he? He doesn't talk about it. I don't even think Briggs and Caleb have talked to him about that time. But maybe he's changed. It's not as if he did anything lately. But we can't completely rule him out just because he gives you orgasms." Arabella winked and came around the car.

Heat crawled up my neck. There were so many times Knight could have hurt me, but he didn't. Just some teasing and name calling the first week. That's all he had done to me.

But what Arabella told me had me doubting his affection.

"I rarely admit this, but I think I was wrong about you and Knight. I think the guy does like you. Every time I showed up at the hospital or at your aunt's place last week, he was there. Waiting like a lonely puppy dog." She shrugged. "Maybe not a puppy dog, more like an affectionate attack dog."

I watched as the valet drove off with Arabella's car. She gripped my good shoulder and leaned in close. "If he does like you, then maybe you can talk to him about his past. He may not open up, but if he sees you care, there's a chance he'll say something."

About the Author

Josie Max is the second pen name for a USA Today Bestselling author. She's a passionate writer of dark heroes, twisted tales, and delicious love stories. Her other passions include reading and coffee. Obviously, she has no life. But that's good, because more time to think up wicked, dark romances with bullying men and fierce heroines. When she's not writing, she's rangling her two little boys and snuggling up with her husband at night so they can pass out from exhaustion together after putting the kids to bed.

www.josiemaxwrites.com

Made in United States
North Haven, CT
19 April 2023